Richard Foreman is the author   e
books, including *Augustus: Son*   f
historical crime novellas. He is also the author of *Warsaw*, a literary
novel set during the end of the Second World War. He lives in
London.

PRAISE FOR RICHARD FOREMAN:

'*Augustus: Son of Rome* forges action and adventure with politics
and philosophy. This superb story is drenched in both blood and
wisdom - and puts Foreman on the map as the coming man of
historical fiction' - Saul David, Author of the *Zulu Hart* series

'Classy, humorous and surprisingly touching tales of cricket,
friendship and crime.' - David Blackburn, *The Spectator*

'A rattling good yarn, requiring only the minimum of suspension
of belief, and leaves one eagerly anticipating the next instalment
of the adventures of the team as they accompany the King to
Harfleur' - Major Gordon Corrigan, author of *A Great and Glorious
Adventure: A Military History of the Hundred Years War*

CONTENTS

RAFFLES:

THE GENTLEMAN THIEF

Chapter One

A tendril of smoke gracefully swirled up from his cigarette into the low-lying, jaundiced fog. Jermyn Street was cast in such a gloom as to be worthy of a scene from Dickens – or Dante. Yet despite the noxious atmosphere – and the gelid air misting up my breath – I could still divine, like a lighthouse in the fiercest storm, the twinkle in my companion's eye. Oh that incomparable, incorrigible, twinkle that had acted as a Siren song – seducing me and nearly dashing me upon the rocks of prison – these recent months.

"We have had stranger jobs, more dangerous jobs, and most decidedly more profitable jobs, my dear Bunny, but I warrant that there have been none so local," Raffles wistfully expressed whilst extracting his trusty skeleton key from the inside pocket of his navy blue woollen blazer.

I briefly considered the proximity of our first 'job' together on that fateful night in Bond Street on the Ides of March, but then nodded in agreement. We were but a few minutes from the Albany, where Raffles resided (when he was not visiting country estates and scoring runs during the day at cricket, and scoring loot at night as a gentleman thief – or I should rather say *the* gentleman thief).

"The ice may not even have melted in your gin and tonic Bunny, by the time we return," Raffles buoyantly added.

The clip-clop of horses and the thrum of a carriage's wheels approached and then rescinded. A party of late-night revellers, either heading to or from a club, could also be heard in the background. With his skeleton key, lifted from a porter at Browns Hotel, Raffles unlocked the back door to Hatchard's of Piccadilly.

"If knowledge is the key to everything Bunny, then this pick-lock runs it a close second," Raffles remarked whilst holding up the skeleton key as it glinted – along with his aspect – in what little light the street offered.

I tightened my sweaty grip around the handle of the black carpet bag which carried the tools of his trade (or rather *our* trade). I then gulped and forced myself through the door, which Raffles courteously held open for me. Fear slithered up and down my spine like an eel. I thought of a thousand things that could go wrong. Even after all this time Raffles had to be confident and courageous enough for the both of us, which thankfully he was.

We soon came through to the back of the shop. I lit our lamp with a match, still trying in vain to noiselessly do so as Raffles could. Tables and shelves of books warmly glowed before us, the gold and silver leaf upon the spines shimmering in the amber haze.

"There are riches here Bunny worth more than those housed in Aladdin's cave," my companion whispered in awe, his eyes feasting upon piled-up volumes of classic titles by Walter Scott, Edgar Allen Poe and Balzac. Raffles was as well-read as he was well-dressed. One was much more likely to find him reading an edition of Byron or Pope than pouring over the society pages or cricket scores even.

A presentiment came over me however, as my gaze found itself inexplicably drawn to a solitary copy of *Crime & Punishment* squatting upon a table – and I cursed the day that I ever set foot across the threshold of 221b Baker Street.

Chapter Two

My heart froze – and then beat like the clappers – as I held the card in my hand.

'Mr Sherlock Holmes requests the company of Mr Harry Manders at 221b Baker St at the earliest opportunity.'

There was an authority in the bold script that transformed the request into a command. The message had been delivered by a wiry, sandy-haired street urchin – no doubt he was a member of Holmes' renowned gang of Baker Street Irregulars. The imp barely disguised his amusement at my perplexed – or just plain terrified – reaction. My face turned as white as the card I was holding and I almost had to ask the youth to lift my jaw up from the depths to which it had dropped. I rubbed my eyes and read the note again, hoping that the burgundy and late night at the baccarat tables were playing tricks upon my mind. A part of me even fleetingly fancied that Raffles might be playing a prank. But this wasn't his style. Also, I knew him to be away. He had been invited to play a game of cricket in Truro. "Normally, I wouldn't play in a match that is so late in the year – but the wish to bowl out the son of our host and then take out his daughter has persuaded me," Raffles explained. "Suffice to say I will not need your assistance for this excursion my friend. The only thing I wish to steal this week is a young woman's heart – and perhaps her virtue," he playfully stated, with a Mephistophelian gleam to his expression.

The ruddy-faced urchin continued to look amused – and expectant.

"Mr Holmes doesn't like to be kept waitin' for a reply mister," the boy eventually piped out, his Cockney accent reminding me of the one Raffles sometimes employed to conceal his true background and breeding.

I was here going to assert that it was presumptuous of Mr Holmes to think that anyone or everyone should drop what they were doing for the day to attend upon him, but I was somehow compelled – or condemned – to reply that I would be able to meet Mr Holmes' request and arrive at Baker Street around noon.

The messenger nodded and thanked me – and then scampered away before I could question him further as to the import of my imminent appointment. I returned to my study and finished off composing an important piece of correspondence, my hand trembling as I signed my name. I tried to commence to write an article, but to no avail. I was far too distracted by the morning's events (and by how the events of the afternoon might unfold). My mind was ablaze with curiosity, but more so worry. Was the game afoot – or game up – for Raffles and I?

Chapter Three

Unable to sit still or concentrate – and wishing to get some air – I decided to leave early and walk to Baker Street. Dr Johnson was perhaps correct in surmising that, 'when a man is tired of London, he is tired of life.' Yet although London is seldom dull, it can often be irksome. Albeit the sky was a vast, oceanic blue with but wisps of cloud breaking up the azure – the scene below the firmament was less serene. Gaudy dresses, shrill voices, equine excrement and seven shades of grime assaulted the senses upon Regent Street. Ill-dressed and ill-mannered tourists conspired to vex me by walking at a slow, obstructive pace – and often travelling upon the wrong side of the pavement. Most of the women out shopping were overdressed and underwhelming, with even the less affluent appearing to have more money than sense. Such was my anxious mood that I resentfully wished to myself that even more of them could discover the joys and freedom of the bicycle, and totter off to the countryside to leave me free to get to Baker Street more expediently.

I pulled my jacket around me tight to trap the warm air in and also to prevent the advances of pickpockets who populate our capital, like vermin must have, during the great plague. I would encourage all gentlemen to put mousetraps in their pockets when shopping along Oxford and Regent Street. I am not sure if this advice may seem hypocritical or ironical given my profession, but mousetraps may do more to stifle petty theft than any well-meaning legislation put forward by our Liberal Party. Oh, if only such devices could snap off the fingers of the taxman too (that far more scurrilous and destructive thief). A hat tax, a window tax and a death tax! What next? Will they soon tax us just for journeying in to London?

I travelled along Oxford Street, marveling at the number of ribbon-strewn window dressers at work, busily changing over their displays in light of the forthcoming festive season. I thought to myself is it me, or is the lead up to Christmas getting longer each year – as our society inexorably slips into serving Mammon instead of God?

I decided to cut through Marylebone. Similar to Bond Street, the prices and intimidating wealth of the area tend to leave the pavements less congested. I sighed and rolled my eyes at witnessing the queue of slack-jawed tourists and our own lower middle-classes snake out of Madame Tussaud's waxwork museum. Marie Tussaud, when alive, created wax figures of the likes of Voltaire, Jean-Jacques Rousseau and Benjamin Franklin. Yet what mediocre and vulgar personalities now populate the museum. I once overheard an eminent social commentator express that 'the exhibits in Madame Tussaud's hold up a mirror to our society.' If so, we should verily be ashamed.

Upon turning into Baker Street I nearly bumped into an esteemed cabinet minister and his companion. Raffles and I had recently encountered the couple at a party (or, for us, it was a job). The cabinet minister was, of course, too important to remember me – or even to apologise to me as he nearly mindlessly knocked me over. I smiled however, upon recalling Raffles' comment at the party in relation to the couple, 'If that is his wife, he should get a mistress. If that is his mistress, he should return home to his wife.'

And so I came to 221b Baker Street, having failed to wholly distract myself during my walk, from the dread I felt at being summoned by the nemesis of every cracksman and criminal in London. I told myself that I could, like Raffles, act a part and be on my way. Yet in the interim of ringing the bell and the door being answered I gulped down two large breaths of free air, in part believing that they could be my last for a while.

Chapter Four

A middle-aged lady with a matronly manner and slight Scottish burr to her accent led me upstairs and into a large sitting room. I am practised at being in the company of very important personages – and in regards to Raffles I am practised at being in the presence of greatness – but nothing could ably prepare me for being casually introduced to –

"Mr Sherlock Holmes and Dr Watson."

Even if I had not been a cracksman's accomplice I would have still stood sheepishly, guiltily, before them I warrant.

A faint, acrid smell of chemicals peppered the air. The curtains were part drawn across the large windows to slash half the room in light and half the room in darkness. I raised my eyebrow and startled a little at seeing a cluster of bullet holes pock-marking the William Morris wallpaper at the far end of the room (Raffles might have satirically argued that the bullet holes improved the pattern). Books, papers, clothes, scientific apparatus and a violin also populated the chamber in a certain ordered chaos. Portraits of Linnaeus and Newton (a not inconsiderable detective himself during his prosecution of the gentleman forger William Chaloner) hung above the fireplace.

Dr Watson hung an elbow upon the fireplace and cleaned out his pipe. He was dressed smartly, but not ostentatiously, in a tweed suit. A solid rugby player's build could still be traced beneath some middle-age spread. He smiled at me and I immediately picked up upon his avuncular character – friendly, trustworthy and not a little unwise.

"Thank you for attending upon us so promptly, Mr Manders."

The head-masterly voice – or it had the richness of an actor's perhaps playing a headmaster – shot through me. Although the greeting was cordial, I still feared for my life (or at least my liberty). The world famous detective sat, or rather was slumped, in a worn leather chair. A tower of newspapers and a coffee table, besmirched with all manner of stains, flanked the chair. Albeit nigh on midday, Holmes was still in his dressing gown. His frame was tall and languid, although there were occasions during our meeting when his body suddenly became as taut and alert as a pointer's. He had a coffin-shaped head and sharp eyes which, unlike his lanky body, were never at rest. His nose was indeed hawk-like and protruded out to such an extent, that I fancied Sherlock Holmes could have smelled tomorrow. His slender fingers were steepled together and his focus seemed to be directed upon wrestling with an abstract problem, as well as dealing with me. Just before he was about to speak again the clock upon the mantle chimed twelve. Holmes and Watson here wordlessly turned to each other and nodded. Watson proceeded to pour two glasses of sherry. There was a sense of familiarity and routine to their behaviour that was akin to an old married couple. Watson offered me a glass but I declined. After pausing slightly, savouring the first sip, Holmes turned his attention to me again. Those two large eyes seemed like shotgun barrels and this Bunny awaited his fate.

Chapter Five

"Now we both know Mr Manders, that I could have you arrested for several counts of burglary."

I gasped and was about to protest my innocence, ignorance and indignation when Holmes just merely shook his head and waved his hand to convey that my protestations would not be worth the effort. I turned my head to the door behind me – and my eyes darted around the rest of the room for any possible escape route should I need one – but Holmes just smiled and shook his head again.

"Please, Mr Manders, There will be no need for flight or fight. If I wanted to put you behind bars I can assure you that you and Mr Raffles would be playing baccarat, using the currency of cigarettes rather than sterling already. Indeed you and Mr Raffles are two of the least likely people I would like to incarcerate – at this present moment in time," Holmes added, looking at me askance as he uttered the last part of this sentence.

"How…how did you guess?" I stammered, infinitely more perplexed and terrified than I had been earlier that morning, upon receiving my summons.

"I never guess. It is a shocking habit – destructive to the logical faculty!" Holmes replied, his body jolting upright in his seat and his tone suddenly reproving. He soon relaxed again however and wryly uttered, "You know a conjurer gets no credit when once he has explained his trick. But suffice to say, a couple of newspaper reports of certain thefts and cricket matches in the same vicinity pricked my interest in Mr Raffles. Inspector Lestrade supplied me with some additional information about the robberies – and then one of my Baker Street Irregulars shadowed Mr Raffles for the day to confirm my suspicions. Thankfully, for you and your friend, I have bigger fish to fry as the saying goes – and I always believed that I would have more use for an amateur cracksman, such as Mr Raffles, this side of the walls of Newgate prison. And it turns out I was correct in that judgement. Besides, my inquiries lead me to believe that Mr Raffles' heart is in the right place – even if the valuables of certain grand families that you and your friend have stayed with are not. Most of those grand families have committed acts of larceny as to make your heists seem venal by comparison however. I am too aware of Mr Raffles' clandestine donations to charity from the fruits of his labours. I also know you to be this Robin Hood's John Little, Mr Manders. Or perhaps you are more so his Alan-a-Dale, recording Mr Raffles' exploits much like Dr Watson here acts as my Boswell?"

I nodded a little and smiled, feebly, to convey to the detective and Dr Watson that his suspicions were, again, correct. I tried to retain my composure but I could feel my heart race and the vein in my neck throb. I wafted up a vague prayer to God in Heaven that all would be well – and also sent out a prayer to Raffles in Truro to come and save me.

Instead of my deliverance though, I was furnished with an offer that I couldn't refuse.

Chapter Six

"What I am about to tell you, Mr Manders, is confidential. It is meant for your ears and those of Mr Raffles alone. You both seem to have the capacity for discretion, given the double lives you have led over recent times. Two days ago my brother Mycroft stood in the very same spot that you are currently occupying. It is rare for my brother to leave his rooms at Pall Mall or his sanctuary in the Diogenes Club, so I was expecting that the reason for his visit was of some urgency and importance."

I could not help but notice the detective's body tense up a little when speaking of his brother, as though his very name could get his haunches up. Dr Watson continued to scour out his pipe and smile at me kindly, as though I were one of his patients. I certainly began to feel like a victim.

"You are a writer by day I believe Mr Manders. We have already deduced your nocturnal vocation. Theafore, I take it that you are familiar with the French author Alexander Dumas and his popular tome, *The Three Musketeers*? For my part I am unfamiliar with such potboilers. I find the plots to be overcooked and the characters contrived."

I here noticed Dr Watson roll his eyes a little in embarrassment and exasperation, and I recalled a line from one of his books, *A Study in Scarlet*, concerning the philistinism of his friend. *'His ignorance was as remarkable as his knowledge. Of contemporary literature, philosophy and politics he appeared to know nothing.'*

"There is a character, one Rene d'Aramis, contained in the novel's pages. As well as being a Musketeer, this Aramis, based upon a genuine historical personage, served as a spy for the French government - and his brief, whilst over in England one summer, was to ingratiate himself into certain circles of the aristocracy. He was able to do so through ingratiating himself into the bedrooms of various wives and mistresses in society. He was, like your Mr Raffles, a gentleman thief, albeit he looked to steal state secrets rather than mere trinkets."

Holmes again looked askance at me, barely disguising his contempt for the common criminal he was addressing.

"He was also, like you Mr Manders, a writer. He kept a journal of his exploits whilst serving over here. He also kept a number of compromising letters written by his conquests. This journal and these letters were given to a lover he was particularly fond of it seems – a mere grocer's daughter rather than duchess – for safe keeping. One of the letters contained in the packet is especially compromising to a current member of our government, as it questions the parentage of one of his antecedents – and therefore brings into question his legitimacy. This letter has recently fallen into the hands of a well-known journalist whose motto is "the truth will out." Before the truth can do such a thing however, it must first be sold to the highest bidder. A newspaper editor – who is a fellow member of the Diogenes Club and who was doubtless an under bidder for the document – brought the issue to my brother's attention. For Mycroft and his Ministry the truth is something to keep in a strongbox, rather than air, like dirty laundry. I must confess that I am indifferent to the fate of the aforementioned minister, but my brother called in a marker and asked me to resolve the situation. I have been charged with retrieving the letter and destroying any provenance of the allegations. Mycroft and his fraternity can be seen to take no part in the affair. I too, am loath to concern myself too much with this trifling matter. I am not my brother's seeker. So I am charging you and Mr Raffles with resolving the situation. I believe that the phrase is considered to be that of 'passing the buck'."

Dr Watson smirked at his friend's usage of an Americanism – his moustache, flecked with grey, curling upwards. I merely remained blank faced and rooted to the spot, like a naughty schoolboy whose headmaster hadn't quite finished disciplining him yet.

Chapter Seven

"Do not be too alarmed Mr Manders, this task is well within your scope. To employ another new-fangled phrase, this extra-curricular excursion will seem like a 'busman's holiday'. I already possess the location of the letter. The journalist has asked a friend of his, the manager of Hatchard's of Piccadilly, to store the letter in the shop's safe. And as to the combination, Mycroft, has called in another favour and furnished us with that information also. The safe is located in the manager's office, behind a portrait of the store's original owner, John Hatchard. I would advise you and Mr Raffles to leave an accoutrement of his trade at the scene and take any money from the safe to disguise the true nature of the break-in. You will of course, pass on any money stolen from the safe – and Dr Watson here will shortly make a large purchase of books from the shop to endow a public library. Please also advise Mr Raffles that should you be apprehended, the blame for the crime must rest on you both squarely. I will deny knowledge of any involvement – and the word of Sherlock Holmes will bowl out for a duck that of Mr A.J. Raffles. Watson, would you kindly give the combination to Mr Manders?"

Dr Watson here handed me a slip of paper containing a set of six digits.

"Now, finally, I wish to convey to Mr Raffles that I am not ordering you to carry out this task. I am no blackmailer, Mr Manders. I am merely asking Mr Raffles to do a good turn for someone who has, by keeping your names out of the newspapers and assizes, done you a good turn. I am asking him a favour, as if I were his brother-in-law – even one who he may dislike for having had an affair. Now, unless you have any questions Mr Manders, our business is concluded."

I stood still in shock and, I think, nodded. I felt lightheaded, like a man who had just been told the date of his execution. I cursed Raffles' absence, as he was my compass and I was all at sea without him. The detective looked at me a little strangely, or scornfully, that I should still be standing there after I had been dismissed – but Dr Watson kindly took me by the arm and led me out. I clasped the top of the banister to steady myself and, before heading down the stairs, caught the following exchange behind the closed sitting room door.

"Do you think that we can trust these fellows with Mycroft's mission?"

"I have every faith in Mr Raffles, Watson, albeit less so his nervous counterpart. Did I ever tell you that I once saw Raffles play at Lord's? He had an arm ball that not even I could rightly detect. But enough of cricket, musketeers and political scandals. We have far more grave concerns. The Napoleon of crime must meet his Waterloo."

Chapter Eight

Raffles returned from Truro the following day. Although I left a message with the doorman of the Albany to ask him to come and see me as soon as possible, with the matter being of the utmost importance, my friend still duly visited his tailor on Conduit Street first and then dropped off his bats into Lillywhite's to be oiled.

My eyes were ringed with sleeplessness and I flustered upon greeting Raffles. I was a heady cocktail of relief and anxiety upon seeing my dear companion's face. Yet despite my hysterical manner (I perhaps appeared more desperate in my behavior than I was even upon the Ides of March), Raffles remained imperiously calm - which in some way heightened my frantic state, believing that he hadn't entirely comprehended the direness of the situation.

"Bunny, sit down and take two deep breaths before you utter another word. All will be well," he finally stated, in both an authoritative and fraternal tone. He proceeded to pour us a large whisky each. He then sat down himself, holding a finger up in the air to convey that I should still desist from speaking (or rather babbling).

"This seems like a two Sullivans predicament," he remarked,

whilst extracting two of his cigarettes from his elegant, engraved silver cigarette case (a gift from his friend and fellow cricketing genius Kumar Shri Ranjitsinhji, or 'Ranji' as everybody called him). "Now, dear Bunny, just begin at the beginning and speak with the economy and clarity of your journalism."

And so I recounted the events of the previous twenty-four hours or so. Raffles interrupted me a couple of times upon points of detail but for the most part he just sat there, receptive and composed. The look on his face was akin to that he wore when playing baccarat, where one had more chance of reading ancient Persian than reading Raffles' reaction to the cards he had been dealt. His sapphire-blue eyes could be the soul of enthusiasm (for cricket, crime, women, poetry) or equally they could prove the soul of insouciance (for all of the aforementioned things also).

A pregnant pause ensued after I finished my report – but then my partner in crime finally responded after taking another sip of whisky and blowing a spiral of smoke up into the heavens, either wishing to choke the angels perhaps, or have them partake in earthly pleasures, too.

"That's good cricket, to request rather than order us to carry out the job," Raffles emitted, shaking his head and smiling as he did so. The gesture resembled that of when Raffles would be bowled by a jaffa. Although slightly melancholy not to get a score, he still couldn't help but admire the ball and wistfully grinned accordingly.

"I had hoped that I would stay off Mr Holmes' telegraph. This is a fine malt by the way Bunny. I regret not being here so as to have accompanied you to Baker Street. Our protector – or prosecutor, depending on which way you look at it – seems a queer fellow. But there is no doubting his brilliant mind. As much as I would have liked to cross wits, as oppose to swords, with him I probably would have, akin to your good self, remained shocked and reverent in his presence. We shall of course assent to his request, partly out of gratitude for not snitching on us these past months. And, as much as I enjoy taking the odd risk and consider myself not without some pluck, I do not wish to make an enemy of Sherlock Holmes. I'm well aware that I play down the order to him in the batting line-up of life.

I downed the rest of my whisky, reckoning that I should start storing up the Dutch courage as early as possible.

Chapter Nine

"We shall carry out the job tomorrow night. Pass me the slip of paper with the combination on it."

And in three seconds Raffles committed to memory that which took me thirty seconds to take in. "If you pack our second choice stethoscope so we can leave it at the scene. Even with our first choice and swathes of luck we probably couldn't crack the safe that way, but the police won't know that. I know we are just dealing with a bookshop, but pack our other tools also. Hope for the best, plan for the worst. I never imagined that I would ever be planning to turn over a bookshop though – and Hatchard's at that. I am very fond of the store and its staff. At least we will have the place to ourselves, Bunny. It'll be a blessing not to bump into the likes of Wilde or Bernard Shaw, accidentally popping in to check the sales of their books or have some fawning American tourist recognise them. Did I tell you I once encountered Ann Radcliffe there? She is able to put a sentence together much better than an outfit. She was wearing a dress that lacked style even when it was in fashion. And we would have needed to use the crowbar you are about to pack to remove her caked on make-up. She asked me if I would like her to base a character in one of her novels on me. I was about to reply that I feared I wasn't one dimensional enough for her work but Wilde came over and rescued me from an awkward moment. It was the first time that I'd ever been grateful for his company. I left them to discuss fashion tips with one another whilst I made my purchases. I bought works by Conrad and Chesterton if I remember correctly. The first, the critics have not been kind enough to – and in regards to the latter they have perhaps been too kind. But I warrant that I am now being as garrulous and as self-centred as an author, Bunny. Tell me more of what you have been up to."

Aside from the events of the past day or so, which I had already relayed, my days since Raffles' departure had been pretty colourless. I had written an article, which would soon be used to stoke someone's kindling. Although I had played some cards and visited Boodles I must confess to you, which I couldn't to my companion, that I had spent most of my time wondering what Raffles had been up to. In regards to Boodles, fellow club members would often come up to me and ask after Raffles – and if I would be meeting him that evening. Upon hearing that he was away, friends would, in various degrees of subtlety, slope off to talk to someone else. I did not blame them. Even I found myself uninteresting – and uninterested – when out of Raffles' orbit. Holmes had called me his Boswell, but yet I also considered myself Sancho Panza to Raffles' Don Quixote. I soon found myself inquiring about my friend's time in Truro. Had he found his Dulcinea del Toboso? Also, I asked him about the cricket.

"My figures were satisfactory. Thankfully the figures of our host's daughter – and her cousin Lucy – were more than satisfactory however," he replied, whilst smiling into his whisky tumbler and stubbing out another Sullivan.

Chapter Ten

Being in the half-light, surrounded by books, reminded me of being back at school again. Part of my duties fagging for Raffles all those years ago, was to fetch books from the library for him after hours. One term he would read the Augustan canon (devouring Horace, Virgil and Ovid), the next term he would apply himself to philosophy (Hume, Locke, Mill). Yet A.J. Raffles would still devoutly consider himself to be a 'lazy' student.

The thick crimson carpet was spongy beneath our feet as we climbed the stairs. Portraits of hoary, disapproving men glared at us from the walls. Finding the pictures and deathly quiet eerie, I turned to my friend and tried to strike up a conversation.

"I wonder which politician is the prospective victim of the letter's contents."

"I doubt that I'll have much sympathy for him, whoever he is. So many of them behave like bastards, whether it be towards their wives or the electorate. Lies trip off their tongues like leg glances off Ranji's bat. There's less fiction in Dumas than there is in their manifestos. A plague on all their houses."

"We are on the third floor, where the shelves of cricket books are," I replied, changing the subject – implying that Raffles might wish to pick out the odd book as a perk of the job.

"I love playing the game dearly old chap, but when not occupying the crease, or bowling at the other end, I try not to think about it. He who knows only of cricket knows nothing of cricket, a sage man once said."

We continued to climb the stairs and reached the top floor offices to the shop. Raffles warmed up his hands, now a little numb from the cold, and removed his skeleton key to open the door to the manager's office. He made easy work of the lock, as if it were the equivalent of someone bowling him a dolly of a full-toss and Raffles cover driving for four. Perhaps we would indeed make it back to the Albany before the ice in my drink melted, I thought to myself. But, as I once overheard Disraeli say at a party, 'Man plans, God laughs.'

Chapter Eleven

The office was relatively small and non-descript, neither religiously tidy nor a mess, neither opulent nor Spartan. I made sure to close the curtains so that not even the slightest crack of light could escape. A large desk, littered in a semi-orderly fashion with invoices and correspondence, dominated the room. A small fireplace sat opposite to the desk.

"It looks like we may well have to pour you another gin and tonic when we get back, Bunny," Raffles exclaimed with a wistful sigh.

He had carefully lifted the accomplished portrait of John Hatchard off the wall, but he was confronted by a locked oak door between him and the safe. Experience – or perhaps the writings of Virgil and Horace – had taught Raffles to remain stoical in the face of such setbacks however.

"It's best you light a small fire to keep us warm while we work. The fog will conceal any plumes of smoke."

I duly lit a small fire, taking pleasure in burning a rival newspaper to that which I wrote for whilst doing so. It soon murmured and then crackled in the background.

We could not pick the lock, nor jemmy the door open. The scene was akin to that of when we broke into the Bond Street jewellers. I stood next to Raffles with a lantern in one hand and rock oil in the other (employed to reduce the noise). This time however, Raffles kept his jacket on as he cut out the lock by drilling a number of holes around it with a brace and bit. Again the holes numbered thirty two in total, albeit where as in Bond Street the task had taken forty seven minutes, Raffles took just forty two to best this door. It was always mesmerising to watch him at work. His being was infused with as much dedication and skill cutting around a lock as when he would carve out a half century at Lord's or the Kennington Oval.

"Thank you, Bunny," he remarked once the door was open. He had little to thank me for, but I was always grateful to be of any assistance. "Now let's see if Mycroft's intelligence is as penetrating as his brother's," Raffles added, smirking at his own pun. "By heavens it is!" he exclaimed with a chuckle as the tumblers clicked into place and the thick steel door squeaked open.

I blew air out of my cheeks in relief. We would soon be back at the Albany. All would indeed be well, as Raffles had promised.

"It doesn't look like there's much money in books," he said whilst extracting a meagre number of notes from the safe. Raffles then quickly sifted through the various papers. He soon found our letter, yellow with age amidst the new white correspondence. Without studying the missive too much he carefully placed it in the side pocket of his jacket. In order not to arouse the suspicion that the safe had been broken into for the letter alone, Raffles also removed a number of other documents (ones which he decided would not inconvenience the store too much if stolen) and gave them to me to stuff into our carpet bag.

The sound of rustling papers was dramatically succeeded however by the unmistakable click behind me of a revolver being cocked. I froze, whilst the eel returned and frantically slithered up and down my spine again. The singular Raffles however merely rolled his eyes, annoyed rather than petrified.

Chapter Twelve

"I am glad that I gave into the temptation to check upon my investment this evening."

The pistol he held was small, but lethal nevertheless. The journalist had an adenoidal voice. Squinting, beady eyes sat over an aquiline nose. An ill-fitting funeral black suit was worn upon a spindly frame. He was not the first journalist I had ever encountered to own both a supercilious and stoat-like air. I just hoped that he would not be the last.

"Put your hands up where I can see them."

I obliged more quickly than Raffles. I must have appeared as pale as the ghost that I was in danger of turning in to.

"Who are you working for? Where is it?" the journalist demanded, rather than asked. His slicked-back, oiled hair was the same shade as the barrel of his gun.

"I don't work for no one but me guv'nor. The score's not been great, but seeing as you're carrying that you can 'ave whatever you want from the box. What is this lark, anyway?"

Doubt and confusion crept into the journalist's haughty expression upon hearing the Cockney accent. As well as his voice

Raffles also mercurially altered his entire posture and manner. I always maintain that the crease's gain was the stage's loss, such was A.J. Raffles' ability to inhabit a role.

"I just want a certain old letter from the safe that you have just cracked. Or my next commission may be to write your obituaries, whether you're working for that conniving peer or some East End thug."

"Old letter? Oh, do you mean this fella?" Raffles replied. He then reached into his jacket pocket and in one swift, but graceful movement, screwed up the paper into a ball and bowled it across the room – and into the fireplace in a perfect arc. If the journalist had been a sports reporter he would have perhaps recognised the smooth and distinctive action, even in the half-light.

Our foe's eyes widened in shock and terror as though someone had just thrown a thousand pound cheque, with the journalist's name upon it, into the flames. He raced to the fireplace to rescue his asset, but before he could do so I ran and rugby tackled him to the ground. He landed with a judder upon the carpet, his attention still fixed upon the ball of paper crimpling and blackening in the fire. The gun spilled from his hand. You may judge that self-preservation had caused me to act so courageously – but more so I was worried that the journalist may have turned his gun upon my friend, in a fit of anger and retribution.

Raffles and I didn't need to tell each other to then bolt out of the door. I pulled on the handle as Raffles quickly used his skeleton key to lock the door and shut the nefarious hack in the office.

"Good work, Bunny," he whispered whilst warmly clasping my shoulder, after the door was secure. "You are worth a thousand John Littles or Alan-a-Dales."

My soul soared upon hearing those words, both at the time of hearing them and now as I recall them.

We ran down the stairs, a mere blur in the eyes of the various portraits hanging upon the walls. Our feet pounded upon the carpet to the same rhythm of the journalist thumping upon the locked office door with his fists. Again, Raffles courteously held the backdoor open for me as we slipped out into Jermyn Street and disappeared into the fog and darkness.

Chapter Thirteen

"Not even Dr Watson himself, when playing for Blackheath Rugby Club, could have tackled that man the way you did this evening old chap," Raffles cheerfully exclaimed as he handed me a freshly poured gin and tonic back at the Albany.

"And not even Dr Grace could have defended the delivery you bowled into the fireplace," I replied – and then clinked glasses with my friend.

All was well. Even the fog outside was dissipating, revealing a bulbous moon and glittering night sky. The fog of cigar smoke infused our elegant but homely chamber however. The clock upon the chimney-piece struck three. I asked Raffles if he would like to accompany me to 221b Baker Street in the morning to tell Sherlock Holmes about the evening's events.

"I am of course tempted, but I would rather keep my distance. It may turn out that Holmes could dislike me – and it'll be Inspector Lestrade, rather than some odious hack, that interrupts us during our next job. Or, perhaps even worse, Holmes may take to me and be compelled to employ us for some future fool's errand. And by Jove that will never do! We're too old to be Baker Street

Irregulars. No, Mr Holmes and I may well meet each other one day – but it will not be in this chapter of my life if I can help it."

"Aye and doing a supposed service to your country isn't the most lucrative of trades," I remarked. "You haven't made any money this week I fear."

Raffles shook his head to dismiss my concern however and asserted,

"Money lost – little lost. Honour lost – much lost. Pluck lost – all lost. Tonight has revealed how you still retain your honour and pluck, Bunny. In another life you could have even been a musketeer. One for all, and all for one."

We proceeded to hold our tumblers aloft and then chimed them together, in the absence of any swords.

Chapter Fourteen

The following day, when I was just about to send a note to Baker Street to arrange a meeting and report upon our success, the sandy-haired Baker Street Irregular descended upon me again like some slightly less than divine Hermes, and informed me that Mr Sherlock Holmes was free to see me at four o'clock that afternoon.

Mrs Hudson, smelling of a mixture of lavender and freshly baked scones, again showed me up to the sitting room. Holmes was again in a dressing gown, albeit of a different design. His hair was unkempt and sprouted outwards in a bird's nest of tangents, as though he had spent the evening tossing and turning in his sleep or scratching his head when awake. His aspect was a little glassy, as though he was being fuelled by a stimulant. He was again sat in his large chair. All manner of newspapers, maps and missives were splayed upon his lap and the arms of the chair, as well as on the table next to him and the floor. His fingertips were stained with so much ink as to make any printer feel deficient.

Thankfully Dr Watson was also in attendance, nestling in an armchair close to Holmes', smoking his pipe contentedly and readying himself with a notepad and pen should Holmes wish his companion to record anything.

The clock upon the mantle chimed four.

"Thank you for your punctuality again Mr Manders. It is an under-appreciated virtue nowadays. You may begin your report. Leave nothing out, although please do not prattle on like the more florid members of your tribe." Holmes did not even look up when addressing me, scrivener-focused as he was upon scanning the sea of papers around him. Reading, filing (it seems there was a system) or discarding the material. Occasionally he would interrupt me with the odd question, such as asking me how large the letter was and which pocket did Raffles store the letter in and how close I came into contact with the document. Upon doing so he would survey my countenance intently, his inquisitive glare burrowing into my eyes – and into my soul. I ended my report by handing the money we took from the safe over to Dr Watson (Raffles had made sure to grab the carpet bag upon exiting the office, whilst still leaving the second choice stethoscope behind).

"Your account tallies with my enquiries. It seems that you have saved the venerated statesman and his recent lineage from ill repute, although I dare say that he will generate a scandal from his own volition sooner rather than later. Without the letter however the journalist will not be able to corroborate his accusations and should any newspaper publish, they will be damned. I feel little sympathy for the journalist in question. Although I am for the freedom of the press, your brethren are not beyond reproach, Mr Manders, and they often trumpet the public interest when the sounds of rapaciousness and tittle-tattle can clearly be heard in the background."

I nodded in agreement at his well-made point, although I dare say I would have nodded in agreement with the fearsome Sherlock Holmes even if I disagreed with him.

"Please pass on my thanks to Mr Raffles. My faith in him was well placed. He is indeed a gentleman and a thief. It seems I may have underestimated you however, Mr Manders. You were uncommonly courageous and quick-witted in a crisis – and Mr Raffles is fortunate to have you as a friend and accomplice. I may not always thank Watson for putting me in the public eye through his colourful stories – but by God I owe him my life and reputation for a number of episodes which remain outside of the public domain. Without him I would be nothing."

Dr Watson here shook his head and coughed a little upon his own pipe smoke.

"Don't listen to him, Mr Manders. When Holmes is not making me red-faced through my exasperation at some of his more peculiar traits, he makes me blush through unwarranted flattery. Enough now, Holmes," Dr Watson gently chided.

I imagined that this was perhaps the closest that the old married couple would ever come to a heated argument.

"I shall not commend you to my brother however. It may spark the idea that he could commission you and Mr Raffles for some future enterprise. How like Mycroft it would be to regularly employ a cracksman to keep, rather than to extract, his skeletons in the closet. Please also pass on to Mr Raffles that I only have a desire to see his name in the papers next to some excellent bowling figures. Although some of his neighbours are doubtless the greatest swindlers in the land, the Albany is still preferable to Newgate."

I again nodded my head.

"Now finally Mr Manders, I wish you to make a promise to me. If ever you or Mr Raffles are summoned to a meeting with a Professor James Moriarty, in lieu of your services, you must vow to make straight for Baker Street before you make your appointment. I have forgiven you and Mr Raffles for past indiscretions, but I will show no mercy should you defy me in this matter. Do you understand?"

I nodded my head more vociferously than ever as Holmes' glare now almost seared a mark upon my soul, so that I would not forget my promise. There was a storm worn upon his brow as he mentioned this Professor Moriarty that made my heart quake. As Raffles could dramatically alter his manner in a second, from brooding to cheerfulness, so too did Holmes here smile and cordially utter –

"Now I believe that concludes our business. That will be all, Mr Manders. I have urgent work to attend to. In regards to that big fish I made reference to frying at our last meeting, we are about to turn up the heat," the detective expressed with relish. "Watson, would you please show Mr Manders out?"

Dr Watson rolled his eyes at the mild inconvenience of getting up and showing me to the door, which was but a few steps away, but he obliged his friend.

"Goodbye Mr Manders."

"Goodbye Dr Watson."

We shook hands and I departed. Mrs Hudson kindly made me a gift of half a dozen scones and some clotted cream as she bid me a good day when I reached the foot of the stairs and she showed me out.

Chapter Fifteen

That same evening I arranged to have dinner with Raffles, partly so I could relay to him the responses of the famous detective to the events at Hatchard's. We were also due to meet C.B. Fry at the Savile Club (of which I had recently become a member) at eleven o'clock. Raffles and I had agreed upon supper in Boodles before that however – and we would first rendezvous at the Albany for a few drinks. Once we were in the company of Fry it would be difficult, for either of us, to get a word in edgeways if he was in a mood to hold court. Yet we both loved 'Charles III' dearly (our nickname for Fry, derived from an article in *Vanity Fair* which titled him thus after recounting all his accomplishments/records as a cricketer, footballer and athlete – whilst still only twenty-one!).

Raffles opened the door with a gin and tonic in one hand - which he passed to me - and a letter in the other. *The* letter!

"By God is that Aramis' letter?!" I ejaculated, nearly spilling my drink as I did so.

"Yes," Raffles responded, as calm as you like – his eyes twinkling as much as any star in the cosmos.

"But how?" I spluttered, this time spilling a little of my drink.

"You see, but do not observe," he wittily replied, quoting a saying of Sherlock Holmes'. "What you saw last night was me tossing into the fire a love letter from Lucy Rosebery, cousin to the daughter of my host over the weekend, rather that of Rene D'Aramis, the musketeer and spy."

"You are a card Raffles, a knave!" I shook my head in slight disbelief and grinned. "You are also as secretive as a spy. Why did you not tell me that you were still in possession of the letter last night?" I tried to be mad at my friend for keeping me in the dark yet again, but I couldn't.

"Elementary, my dear Bunny. Holmes' hawk-like nose would have smelled a rat should you have tried to lie to him about the letter going up in flames. You are too honest for your own good sometimes, but I would not want you any other way my friend."

"What will you do now with the document?"

"Nothing. Like Holmes, I'm no blackmailer. I will keep the letter to use as a bargaining chip should we ever get pinched. I'll place it in a safety deposit box tomorrow. As long as we never have to darken a courtroom, the letter will never see the light of day," he issued, placing the paper upon his desk for him to attend to in the morning.

I here asked Raffles if it was wise to try and out-fox Holmes, but that incorrigible twinkle which lit up Jermyn Street returned to his expression and he gamely exclaimed,

"A man's reach must exceed his grasp, dear boy, or what the dickens is a heaven for?"

Over a couple of drinks I went through my meeting with Holmes and Dr Watson. Upon finishing Raffles savoured the taste of his Sullivan, drained his whisky and announced,

"Now, let us draw a line under the events of the past few days, close the chapter. It seems that we are, blessedly, small fry for Holmes. Make Mrs Hudson's scones last Bunny, for God willing you will not have cause to visit 221b Baker Street for some time. We will keep our promise though, if ever this Professor Moriarty gets in touch." Raffles glanced at his pocket watch and added, "But let us now visit Boodles, before they run out of the duck terrine or John Dory."

Chapter Sixteen

Most of the remainder of our evening passed without incident, aside from some gangly drunk bumping into Raffles outside the Albany and our waiter at the club spilling half a glass of Pol Roger over my new trousers. It was a night for clumsiness, in more ways than one.

Unfortunately, Raffles' fears were realised in that the club had but one serving of the duck terrine left by the time we arrived – which he insisted that I have. The John Dory had completely finished however, but we could compliment the sommelier upon his choice of claret to go with our lamb. If only I could compliment our waiter on his steady hand. As was the case in most instances when Raffles dined at the club, he was approached by either friends or fans complimenting him on his cricket season, or inviting him to play at their houses the following season. Raffles always gave a cordial, but non-committal reply.

In between courses I asked my friend about Lucy Rosebery. I was normally chary in inquiring about Raffles' affairs, as I envisioned that one day he would inform me that he had found his intended, and our life of crime – and gentlemanly conviviality

– would be over. But I was curious about this young woman who had written a love letter to Raffles so soon after they had first met.

"Although I ventured to Truro to, in part, court her cousin Margaret, I found myself spending an increasing amount of time in Lucy's company – and missing not Margaret as I did so. She is uncommonly pretty Bunny, with a slim figure hewn from vigorous exercise rather than under eating. Her long blonde tresses seem spun from gold and her blue eyes, unlike how mine can sometimes be, are never cold. She has something about her my friend, a quality. Or should I say qualities? Aye, she has honour, pluck – and money," he enthused. Such was the mischievous gleam in his aspect that I discerned not how much weight he attached to this last asset. Even after all these years there were times when I could still only read Raffles about as well as I could pick his off break.

"Unfortunately she has recently joined the suffragettes, but nobody's perfect. But for all of her spirited and modish opinions about emancipation and the lower classes she still possesses an old fashioned grace and charm. Put simply, she doesn't bore me Bunny. I am inclined to see her again, when she comes down to London next month. I'm unsure as to whether she's intending to save womankind or the lower classes during her week here, but hopefully she will also make time to save this scoundrel. But do not worry, the champagne is not going to my head – far more was spilled over your new trousers. I have not lost my heart to Ms Rosebery. I am still much more likely to wear the ball and chain of Newgate, to that of matrimony. But what of you old chap –

any news?"

My news and conversation always seemed to pale in comparison with Raffles', but I mentioned how the *Strand Magazine* had asked me to write a piece on London's bookshops. Are they leaders or followers of taste?

"Fry has also just been sounded out on whether he wants to write some articles on football and cricket for them. He wants my advice, having written for the Strand before. I will tell him to go ahead. The magazine is not just full of the kind of potboilers that Mr Holmes derides so much."

I was here interrupted by a waiter, who brought over to the table two of the club's famous Orange Fools.

"But what of your next job?" I remarked in a hushed tone, unable to suppress my sense of intrigue and excitement however.

"The game is afoot on that score my friend – and again the job will be close to home. Indeed it couldn't be closer. But let me leave it there for now."

Shortly afterwards the clock struck ten. We ordered two small ports whilst asking for the bill.

"As much as he won't be short of company, or rather an audience, we should head over to the Savile to meet Fry soon. I can picture him now, showing members the perfect cover drive using an umbrella as a bat and an apple for a ball." Raffles joked.

"I agree. We would not want to miss the final act to our evening."

The waiter brought over our ports and the bill. I went to sign the chit but Raffles held up his hand.

"Please, it's on me, old chap. I insist. You can get the drinks at the Savile."

Raffles reached into his inside pocket for a pen. He rummaged around in slight befuddlement. I was about to ask if he had mislaid his wallet when he placed the item upon the table. A pen too materialised. Yet still he continued to search for something on his person. He checked all of his pockets twice, thoroughly. It was rare for that smooth, handsome brow to be creased in concern. His blue eyes even lost their lustre, as if put out by a blunt instrument. He then just paused and pensively shut his eyes, as if replaying a memory.

"What's wrong, my friend?" I asked, perturbed in sympathy.

"I have a horrible suspicion that the final act of this evening could now prove tragic," Raffles remarked cryptically, as much to himself as to me. He quickly signed off on the bill, leaving a far too generous tip for our dunderhead waiter.

"Come Bunny, we must make straight for the Albany."

Chapter Seventeen

The rain first coughed down upon us when leaving the club in St James', but by the time we reached Piccadilly the heavens opened. I nigh on had to run to keep pace with my friend, who strode on like a man possessed, his overcoat billowing in the snarling wind. When retrieving our coats from the cloakroom of the club I had questioned Raffles again on the dramatic change in his behaviour.

"I do not wish to yet say anything Bunny, for fear of appearing paranoid or fantastical. But by God, this is the night that either makes me, or forgoes me quite. Reynard may have well been out-foxed."

The rain chilled my already bloodless pate as we dodged around hansom cabs and weaved through the sodden throng occupying the pavement. I began to wish that I was in possession of my revolver, such were my foreboding thoughts. I warrant that there had been times when Raffles had run between the wickets with less urgency, compared to how he marched on now down Piccadilly. He began to mutter to himself,

"When you have eliminated the impossible, whatever remains, *however* improbable, must be the truth... But not even I would have taken such a risk."

We were greeted at the entrance to the Albany by the ever-amiable doorman Clarence, who made some comment about the weather. Yet – and this is the only instance I can remember of my friend ever being discourteous to the staff of the building – Raffles ignored the man and bounded up the stairs, three steps at a time.

I was panting heavily – and Raffles looked as if he were about to snort fire – as he opened the door to his apartment and rushed to his desk.

"The devil! The rogue!" Raffles exclaimed, striking the antique walnut bureau (which had once been the property of Coleridge). Mystification and concern vied for sovereignty in my being.

"The fiend! The genius!"

As I tentatively approached my friend his anger began to mercurially transform into amusement – and admiration. Rather than pound his beloved bureau, he now slapped his desk in celebration, or congratulations. The congenial twinkle returned to his aspect, like the sun coming out from behind the clouds.

"The gambler! The poet!" he trumpeted, before filling the air with sweet laughter. I couldn't help but grin too in sympathy, albeit my relief was still allied to being mystified.

"We have been humbugged Bunny, by the Napoleon of Justice! Our loss of the letter – and the immunity from prosecution it may have provided – is offset by the fact that we may well be immortalised one day by Dr Watson. The drunk, who nigh on knocked me over outside the Albany this evening, was none other than Holmes! He pick-pocketed me, relieving me of my skeleton key – which he then used to break into my apartment. The man is a marvel. Perhaps I should have heeded your advice and placed mousetraps in my pockets."

Again he laughed, clapping me on the shoulder.

"Look, there upon the desk Bunny. I dare say that I will treasure his note more than any written by our monsieur Aramis."

Moving aside the skeleton key which lay upon it, I picked up the note. Perhaps it was the cold, but my hands trembled a little in excitement - or trepidation.

'*It takes a thief to catch a thief. S.H.*'

I smiled.

RAFFLES:

BOWLED OVER

Chapter One

It was shortly after the affair with Sherlock Holmes and the Rene d'Aramis letter. Russet and yellowing leaves swirled around in the breeze and occasionally slapped upon the windowpane. Although it was a bright, crisp autumnal day I stood in Raffles' apartment in the Albany and lit a candle. I would often do so when he was away (Raffles was visiting Ranji and Fry in Sussex; I had been invited too, but alas I had a couple of deadlines to meet). He would give me a set of keys and allow me make use of his extensive library and superior cellar of clarets and chardonnays – and in return I would do him the favour of keeping a candle alight upon his desk. When I was unavailable to do so he would charge a member of staff in the building to carry out this task, or ritual. If the staff thought him eccentric by way of this quirk, heaven knows how they would have viewed Raffles if they knew of his nocturnal exploits as an amateur cracksman. When I infrequently asked him as to why he kept a lighted candle upon his beloved walnut bureau (it had once belonged to Samuel Taylor Coleridge) Raffles would merely reply that he would 'tell me one day'. Suffice to say I was used to my good friend keeping me in the dark, even in the presence of a glowing taper.

Upon lighting the long, thick candle – using the old one still burning on the desk to do so – I could not help but notice a letter upon the bureau, addressed to one Lucy Rosebery (a young woman who Raffles had recently met whilst in Truro, playing cricket). Although I am not usually one to snoop – a queer assertion one might think, given the fact that I serve part-time as a cracksman's accomplice – I surrendered to curiosity and surveyed the letter. 'Tis a poor excuse, but I told myself that Raffles had invited me to be his biographer (of sorts) and the more source material I had, the better.

Dear Lucy,

Thank you for your letter. Its scent still perfumes my breast pocket – as similarly the sweet memories of our time spent together in Truro linger. I can still picture your fair and lively features, framed by your golden ringlets, as we sat in the garden and you told me about your childhood, your plans for the future and your fondness for the novels of Miss Austen. You are like no other woman I have ever met.

I dearly hope that all is well with you. I know that you are ever conscious of dressing stylishly but please do also dress up to meet the changes in the seasons, as well as the changes in fashion. I will be sick at heart myself if you are taken ill and unable to visit London soon.

I must ask you to promise that you keep our correspondence – and dare I hope courtship – secret for now. Please do not tell your cousin, especially. I spent some time with her also whilst in Truro and I would not wish her

somehow resenting you, or me, in that I cherish your affections more. So too
I would prefer if we could spend our time alone in the capital, rather than
with your cousin or friends.

I will write again soon. You are the last person I think about at night –
and the first I think of in the morning.

Raffles

I drew in a breath and was just about to ponder how my consummate bachelor friend could be falling in love when I noticed a similarly worded letter, addressed to Margaret (Lucy's cousin), upon the desk also. I half-smiled, yet also shook my head disapprovingly. "All life should be considered as sport Bunny," my hero sometimes glibly asserted. Blinded by his twinkling but unreadable blue eyes, as well as a charmingly disarming grin, I was ever unsure as to how sincere Raffles was when expressing this cynical philosophy – knowing how noble his heart could be also.

Chapter Two

Raffles returned the following day – and that evening he asked me to accompany him to a party being held by one of his neighbours in the Albany. You may well already be familiar with the figure of Rupert Robert Fuller but should you have the good fortune to be oblivious to this blight upon humanity, I have inserted below part of an article that a journalist friend of mine wrote about him, shortly before the night of his party.

'...*After his self-proclaimed 'conquest' of the United States of America the merchant banker Rupert Robert Fuller has returned to our shores. America's gain is Britain's loss. This progeny of Dickens' Josiah Bounderby and the Whore of Babylon has moved in to the Albany and will be throwing himself a welcome home party in a fortnight's time (presumably because no one else is fond enough of the financier to arrange a homecoming celebration for him). The usual suspects will doubtless be in attendance. Fuller is never shy in asserting which politicians he has in his pocket – and which newspaper editors and celebrities are keeping them company in there, along with his diamond encrusted money clip. His acolytes, sucking upon the teat of his oozing wealth, would make Talleyrand, or even Tamerlane, seem principled. Fuller purchases influence and people as if he were buying a new hat. And he might well need a new hat for his hair has thinned, whilst his waist has expanded considerably since his extended business trip across the Atlantic. "The stakes are high," he remarked before setting sail. Now back, he perhaps can attest that, also, "the steaks were large". Boodles have recently placed a Trojan Pig on their menu, in anticipation of Fuller dining there and enjoying his favourite dish. If the waiters at the club do not sense him coming, with the ground suddenly starting to tremble beneath their feet from Fuller's rotund build, they will still no doubt see him coming from afar. Our modern day Crassus is famed for his over-sized bejewelled cufflinks and tie-pins... Rupert Robert Fuller will tell you that he was an Oxford Blue, that he holds college records for the one and two hundred yard sprints – and that he possesses bowling and batting figures to make a mortal out of the good Dr Grace even. The record books will tell a different story however - but the financier was never one to invest in the commodity of the truth when a boast could suffice. The plutocrat (but oh, what he would not give to be an aristocrat!) is forever reminding everyone of his humble background – and the fact that he is 'self-made' as opposed to having inherited his wealth. His parents indeed never provided their son with any serious capital, but he was however bailed out from bankruptcy and financed by his affluent aunt and uncle throughout the early stages of his career. His failures in business were as numerous as those on the cricket field, to begin with... His break came through investing in a gold mine in Australia, which was found to house greater deposits than originally thought. The self-titled 'Prophet of Profits' will fail to mention however that he was on the cusp of selling his share in the mine before the new deposits of gold were discovered. From then on, money made money – with even two divorces failing to stymie his gluttonous empire… To adapt a quote from Punch magazine Rupert Robert Fuller is worse than wicked, he's vulgar.'*

Although a new neighbour – and Raffles could be a prince of politeness, as well as a prince of thieves – I was still a little surprised that my friend would wish to associate himself with someone of Fuller's ilk and accept his invitation to the party. Especially as, after first encountering the financier, he said of Fuller that he was both 'boorish and boring'. Before the party, Raffles and I had a couple of drinks in his apartment and I raised the issue.

"My dear Bunny," he replied, whilst picking a small piece of fluff off the lapel of his dinner jacket, "I am not attending the party this evening to swell my social circle – but rather to swell my bank balance. Far more than any crony or caterer at the gathering tonight, I will be working."

I coughed, nearly choking upon my gin and tonic, and marvelled at the mischievous gleam which shone in my friend's aspect, lighting up the room far more than any candle.

Chapter Three

Before venturing upstairs Raffles briefed me further. We would not be making our play this evening. Rather our task was just to reconnoitre the apartment, its valuables and our host.

"I mean to fillet our bloated catfish more than either of his ex-wives' lawyers, but not tonight old chap. Just keep your eyes and ears open."

We both rolled our eyes upon seeing the throng of guests outside of Fuller's apartment. I nodded, smiled politely and said hello to a number of people in the queue who I neither knew, nor wanted to get to know. Conversely I believed that once they knew who I was they would cease to wish to get to know me also.

"I never realised that so much vacuity could fit into just one room," Raffles drolly confided to me upon entering the party, whilst arching his eyebrow and pursing his lips. He then took a breath, as if he were about to go on stage, and smiled – ready to radiate charm.

Crystal chandeliers and jewellery sparkled through the haze of cigarette smoke. The drinks were long, whilst the skirts upon the young women serving them were short. Perhaps Fuller did indeed possess the Midas touch – and he had spent the afternoon fingering half of his furniture – such was the influence of gold and gilt upon the decor. The apartment dripped with opulence, rather than style. The tastelessness could be summed up in one word – Harrods. A magazine editor had recently asked me to write a story on the Brompton Road store, or more precisely its new moving staircase (or 'escalator' as I have heard one fellow call it). Patrons were offered a brandy at the end of their 'moving experience' (whether this was offered as a reward or for medicinal purposes I was not quite sure). My brandy was downed in one however upon witnessing the arabesque aesthetic – and prices of the ghastly pieces – when reaching the top of the stairs.

"Raffles, darling," a voice screamed out. Such was its high-pitched squeal that I was worried that my champagne glass might crack. I had only just recently cleaned my trousers from having champagne spilled over them by a clumsy waiter at Boodles. At least, on that occasion, I had the distinction of being marked by good champagne.

The woman behind the shrill greeting was Celia Woodeville, an actress. She and Raffles may well have had an affair in the past. Celia was renowned for her weight fluctuating more than Fuller's stock portfolio. Celia was getting to the age where she was more likely to play Gertrude than Ophelia – and so she now dressed like a woman half her age and displayed twice the youthful exuberance that she should have to in order to compensate. Whether encountering Celia on or off stage I could not call myself a fan. The asp was kinder than the critics were when she played Cleopatra – and she died on the stage long before the final act when playing Cordelia. Yet the slightly fading English rose still kept herself in work. She also often kept herself in the newspapers, mainly through having a string of suitors who became increasingly younger as she grew older. She would soon be picking up her lovers from the playground, rather than the nightclubs.

"Celia, it has been too long. How have you been?" Raffles asked as she sided up to us both, albeit she soon turned her back on me.

"Well I do not particularly want to re-live it but did you not hear about the drama at Rupert's estate upon the Isle of Wight?"

"It's fine if you do not wish to speak about it."

"It's almost too horrible to describe, or too impossible to explain, but there was an awful fire! I found myself rescuing Rupert's great aunt from her room and guiding her downstairs to safety. It was terrifying. I can barely bring myself to talk about it. Did you not see my interview in *the Telegraph* about the incident?"

Our drama queen took a frantic breath and was on the cusp of recounting the entire ordeal when, thankfully, she gazed over Raffles' shoulder and espied an eminent theatre critic and producer. She swiftly excused herself and fluttered over to the pair, squealing someone else's name – a moth attracted to a brighter flame.

"That was a lucky escape," I remarked and sighed.

"Aye, I think I would have preferred the company of the aunt – or fire even. I fear age has withered her, Bunny," my friend said a little ruefully.

Chapter Four

Raffles had decided beforehand that, in order to glean more information about our quarry, we should spend most of the evening apart. My friend soon swapped my company for that of a pretty maid. When she wasn't blushing at one of Raffles' compliments, her heart-shaped face bloomed with freckles. I knew however that his flirting would be but a prologue to subtly put questions to her about the household and her employer. The lines were often blurred between work and play for A.J. Raffles.

I found myself in the company of an old journalist friend however, who possessed bags under his eyes rather than freckles. I had positioned myself close to the horseshoe of guests surrounding our host. They laughed at Fuller's witticisms (for want of a more derogatory term) as if Dan Leno were performing. The lines seemed blurred between where Fuller's porcine features met his chin (or chins) and neck. His black, oiled hair desperately yearned to cover most of his scalp – yet failed. Stubby fingers clasped an equally stubby cigar and his blood-red ruby cufflink shone in the light as he held it aloft. In between raspy guffaws and loud hums of agreement I caught the following dollops of oratory.

"When I first entered the City I thought, much like Pompey did when thinking about becoming the First Man of Rome, that if Sulla could, why can't I? ...A shark is born swimming... I haven't got the time to read anything... I dare say I pay about as much tax as the poor doorman to Albany. And my new address is Albany rather than *the* Albany. The unrefined and ill educated refer to it as the latter... Indeed my ex-wives have proved far more taxing than any government, thanks to my accountant. A piece of advice gentlemen – you should pay yourself in shares and cash bonuses. I also possess more bank accounts than tie-pins. In some ways I also own more banks than most people possess tie-pins."

A chorus of laughter again rang out amidst clouds of cigar smoke. Rupert Robert Fuller's bombast and self-love here reminded me of Reuben Rosenthall – and a chill ran down my spine as I briefly recalled the scene of being apprehended whilst breaking into Rosenthall's house. I was shot at by the brute – and only saved from prison or the mortuary through Raffles dressing up as a constable and leading me off. The full story is recounted in *A Costume Piece*.

"I am surprised to see you here old chap," my journalist friend, Thomas "Arrows" Fletcher remarked, snapping me out of my reverie.

"I've come as a guest of Raffles, who lives downstairs. I am a little surprised to see you here, too. Not usually your patch."

Like myself Arrows was a hack, albeit he was a crime reporter. We may have dressed well and have been courted and admired

in some quarters – but in truth we were no higher on the
Elizabethan chain of being than an accountant or a used hansom
cab salesman. Indeed there are some from our tribe who rank
little above a jackal or leech.

"There are more crooks in here than at the Old Bailey, don't
worry about that. But my editor insisted that I attend and pay
court to the would-be Rockefeller. I have to write a diary piece.
Needs must, Bunny. At least the food is better than most of the
company here, which is not to say that the food is good."

As ever, Arrows had hit the mark.

Chapter Five

What more can I say about the party? Firstly, our host gave a speech.

"Thank you all for coming this evening. I see many dear friends before me. Dearer to me still, are the investors I see. And even dearer to me are those people here who owe me money. You should know that should we all be aboard a sinking ship right now, I would toss my friends overboard in an instant to save those who are indebted to me. But we are far from being a sinking ship, do not worry. You are as safe with me are you are with the Bank of England... It's also nice to see so many members of parliament here. But it's unsurprising. Parties held by bankers are always more entertaining – and influential – than political parties...,"

Sycophantic laughter accompanied most of Fuller's comments. His accent was a strange mixture of Home Counties, east coast American and Australian. His tone was also imbued with menace, as well as humour.

I deliberately got lost trying to find my way to the bathroom, in order to reconnaissance more of the apartment. I was also later cornered by a zealous H. G. Wells, who showered me with spittle and theories as to how eugenics could solve all of mankind's ills. "Germany is far more progressive in its attitude towards the science," Wells passionately argued whilst waving a bread stick in the air, as if he were conducting an orchestra. "In the absence of God, man must become a god!" he added. If only eugenics could breed out evangelical atheism, I thought to myself.

It came as a welcome relief when Raffles gestured that we should leave. When saying goodbye to Celia Woodeville she got my name wrong. I was too tired or embarrassed to correct her – and besides she would neither remember me as 'Bunny' or 'Binny' the next time we meet. Being too late to have supper at Boodles or the Savile we headed downstairs for a nightcap at Raffles' apartment.

My friend was soon ensconced in his favourite armchair, cradling a whisky and soda-water in one hand and holding a cigarette in the other.

"I could not but help be reminded of a quote by our neighbour this evening, Bunny," Raffles remarked, accurately flicking ash into an ashtray several inches away. The 'neighbour' Raffles referred to was Lord Byron, who had lived in the apartment next to his at the Albany when he was a young man.

"Which one?" I asked, tipsily missing the ashtray from an inch away.

"Society is now one polished horde,
Formed of two mighty tribes – the bores and bored."

Chapter Six

"So what did you find out about our prey this evening old chap?" Raffles asked, leaning back in his chair, his eyes half closed in either thoughtfulness or tiredness.

"I discovered that he's even more odious and vulgar than I first considered. Our banker upstairs is certainly no George Peabody. I will assist you in any way I can to help clip his wings. No matter how much we relieve him of though I dare say that the camel will still not be passing through the eye of a needle. He possesses some works of art that are worth stealing, albeit not keeping. But there's definitely fruit upon the bough, ripe for the picking. Talking of which, I saw you conversing a fair bit to that maid throughout the party. Was that business or pleasure?" I remarked, with my eyebrow arched in either quizzicality or suggestiveness. I think the drink emboldened my spirits in regards to prying.

"Both," my friend replied. His eyes were now awake and gleaming, his mouth curled in a charming smirk.

"She is pretty."

"She is more than pretty, Bunny. She was probably the most decent and admirable creature at the party. Her name is Mary

Flanagan. As well as working as a maid she is training to become a nurse. She comes from a family of close to a dozen and they all live south of the river in a tenement building in Bermondsey. She is free from complaint or affectation. She has a wit which bestraddles both the earthy and satirical. She quoted both Ruskin, 'there is no wealth but life', and Milton, 'what good is strength without double the wisdom', during our conversation. When I enquired as to the school she attended Mary blushed and replied that she had just visited the library a lot."

I had oft heard my friend speak of other women in a similarly effusive manner, yet even so there was a singular enthusiasm in his tone when speaking about the young maid. Indeed, I had heard Raffles speak about more dishes over the years than even Mrs Beeton collected in her famed cookery book. Yet this Mary Flanagan had stirred a sense of intrigue, as well as attraction, in him.

"Are you smitten with her? Will you see her again?" I asked. I was calm inside, yet eager to know his intentions. I was often fretful that Raffles would choose a wife and that our life of leisure – and crime – together would come to an end. I was half disapproving, but half pleased, whenever Raffles would casually seduce and then disregard such creatures as Lucy Rosebery and Mary Flanagan.

Raffles sat back in his chair again, his aspect still bright though wreathed in cigarette smoke. He paused before answering, but then finally spoke whilst staring up at the ceiling – as if he were looking up to the heavens for instruction or inspiration.

"No. Society would say of any match that I am too good for her. Yet Society – and not for the first time - would be wrong, Bunny. She is too good for me. But that could just be the drink talking."

Chapter Seven

I worked from home the following morning, although my mind dwelled upon a slightly different job in prospect. When I had asked Raffles as to what he had learned about the banker he replied,

"I ascertained the first valuable piece of knowledge about Fuller before this evening. That being that he carries his keys in his overcoat pocket whenever he ventures out. The second piece of information, which I discovered tonight from Mary, is that Fuller will be throwing another party, just for his City associates, on Friday night. In marrying these two pieces of intelligence together I think I have come up with the offspring of a plan, old chap."

Frustratingly, yet typically, Raffles declined to divulge his plan further. I think it amused him to keep me in the dark and see me shocked, scared or confuted during our escapades together. Should you somehow consider this behaviour cruel or callous, know that I believed that Raffles would never betray or abandon me – and would rather sacrifice in an instant his well-being for my own.

I spent part of the afternoon in the London Library, in the hope of getting some work done there. But the place was populated by numerous other scribblers – and the stacks became a hive of gossip rather than industry. Instead of being a crucible to discuss a wealth of knowledge, people cattily discussed the wealth of others in regards to how much those absent from the library that day were being paid for their work.

Arrows and I had arranged to have supper that evening, but I got to the Old Bailey early to sit in on a couple of cases that he was covering. All human life could be seen at the court, unfortunately. The first case involved a protracted suite to rival that of Jyndyce and Jyndyce. I had been an observer to such cases before. Justice, if we can prostitute the term as such, would go to the party who could afford the best lawyer. Little has changed in some ways since the days of Cicero and Hortensius. When the case finally ended six months or so later I read that the winning party had claimed that 'Justice had prevailed.' I rather think, instead, that it was the lawyers who had come out on top.

The second case involved an insurance fraud. The defendant, one Edward Salter, an estate agent from Barnes, was arguing that his governess had robbed him of his wife's jewellery. The lawyer acting for the insurance company however refuted the defendant's version of events and built a case based upon the estate agent's past misdemeanours. "Produce an honest estate agent before me in this court and I'll produce Jack the Ripper." He also sardonically made reference to the 'mysterious' governess, who no one could locate. "She is perhaps as great a fictional governess as Jane Eyre," the leather-faced prosecuting attorney posited. "Or, in that this Miss Finnigan has gone missing, perhaps we should be trying the defendant for kidnap as well as insurance fraud." Although entertained by the droll, veteran of the court his audience here looked dimly across at the estate agent. I warrant that Arrows could have written up the outcome of the trial there and then, without having to hear any official verdict.

We suppered at the Reform Club, where Arrows is a member. H.G. Wells was on an adjacent table and one couldn't fail to hear him preaching about the virtues of science and eugenics again. It wasn't hard for my steak tartare to prove more palatable than his progressive views. The evening was part business, part pleasure, as I was conscious of winkling out any additional information that my friend might possess in regards to Fuller.

When I casually asked about the financier Arrows screwed his face up in distaste, as though his Dover Sole had been over seasoned.

"If it's mathematically possible, Fuller furnishes his profession with an even baser reputation than it deserves. I have known serial perjurers to behave more honestly, Bunny," Arrows exclaimed, whilst slicing into his fish with more vigour than was necessary. "I am reminded of a quote by Mark Twain. 'A banker is a fellow that lends you an umbrella when the sun is shining and wants it back the minute it begins to rain.' Yet it seems that Fuller has failed to save for a rainy day – and his backers in the United States may want their umbrella back. Rumour has it he is over leveraged and the reason why he returned to London is that the Americans were about to seize certain assets. Whether a prince or a pauper, one should always heed Mr Micawber's advice. 'Annual income twenty pounds, annual expenditure nineteen pounds nineteen and six, result happiness. Annual income twenty pounds, annual expenditure twenty pounds ought and six, result misery.'"

I nodded my head in agreement and washed down my steak with a mouthful of vintage claret that I could ill afford.

Chapter Eight

The following day I ventured over to the Albany, picking up a jar of Raffles' favourite caviar – and also a tin of their Heinz baked beans – at Fortnum & Mason beforehand. I treated myself to some of their excellent foie gras – and the original producer of the Scotch egg is still the best. I had arranged to meet Raffles for lunch, where I hoped he would reveal more of his plan for the imminent job. Yet when I knocked upon his door, just after midday, someone other than my friend answered it.

"Good afternoon. You must be Mr Manders. Or can I call you Bunny, or Harry?"

For a fleeting second or so I did not recognise the young woman – and I was confused, or rather bewitched. I had certainly not heard her voice before which, though relatively well to do, also betrayed echoes of an Irish brogue and Cockney.

"I'm Mary. Mary Flanagan," she added, whilst smiling warmly and opening the door to let me in.

Brown, satin boots poked out beneath a long, pleated blue skirt. She also wore a long-sleeved, high-necked cream blouse fastened with mother of pearl buttons. There was something stylish, yet anonymous, about her outfit as though it could have been a maid, or mistress of a house, standing before me. The dark red lipstick she was wearing gave her mouth a fuller, more sensual quality. The colour matched her strawberry blonde – and slightly dishevelled – tresses. Her eyes, like Raffles', were playful and intelligent. For a moment or two the young woman surveyed me intensely, but then her expression and manner relaxed again.

"Raffles is just getting dressed. Would you like a drink whilst you wait?"

I was taken aback somewhat by her ease of manner – and perhaps I felt a little proprietorial in that I often played the host and fixed the drinks whenever Raffles had guests. I could find the gin bottle in the apartment blindfolded (I was unsure whether to be proud of this ability or not).

"I will have a gin and tonic. Thank you."

I couldn't help but just dumbly stare at the young woman, who seemed mature beyond her years. There was a grace to her movements, but I also sensed a potential wildness to her being as well – as though she were a tigress about to pounce.

"Raffles is extremely fond of you. In some ways he even envies you – for your decency and modesty. I think you help save him from himself. Yet even on a glorious summer's day, with Raffles at the crease, I fancy one could still only see a shadow of him. Should I have known him for all of his life, rather than just for a few days, I still could not say that I wholly understand him. He is always in the half light."

"He defies augury," I stated – fishing to see if the unschooled young woman would understand the literary reference.

"Nothing is good or bad in relation to Raffles, but thinking makes it so," she quickly replied, grinning sphinx-like as much to herself as at me.

I thanked her as she handed me my gin and tonic. I sat down in my usual chair and just politely smiled, feeling a touch awkward also. Unlike Raffles I was uncomfortable in the company of the lower classes. I often found myself pitying them, or finding them alien, scary or contemptible. Although I could not quite say that I felt these things when in the company of Miss Flanagan – she defied her class or classification – I still remained subdued. I craned my head to peer up at the sky out of the window, creasing my face slightly in expectation of rain. I also took multiple sips from my drink and looked everywhere around the room, aside from at the intimidatingly beautiful woman whose company I was in.

"I think perhaps that Raffles feels a little guilty, in that he has somehow taken advantage of me. I do not want you to think Bunny that I have somehow taken advantage of him. Raffles speaks oh so well of you – and I have read many of your pieces. When it comes to it please tell him –"

She broke off what she was saying upon hearing Raffles enter the room. He was dressed in a well-cut black suit and crisp white shirt. I reminded myself that I should take up Raffles' offer of arranging for the Albany to look after my laundry and ironing. "Not even your own mother would iron your clothes with such attention and pride," Raffles had proffered. Not that either of our mothers ever did any laundry or ironing.

"Afternoon Bunny, I am sorry to have kept you waiting, although I am glad that you have been able to meet Mary in the interim. Now are you sure that you would not like to join Bunny and I for lunch?"

"I'm sure. You boys go off and play in your tree house. I have things that I must attend to. I cannot afford to take another day – and night – off from my work and studies," she replied with a sly, but far from unsubtle, look upon her face as she addressed Raffles. The spirited young woman then pinned up her fiery tresses in a blaze of industry and elegance – and fixed her bonnet upon her head in the mirror (the style of which seemed beyond the pay of a mere serving maid, yet I surmised that Raffles had taken her shopping on Bond St, as was his custom to do). When Raffles kissed the cheek of the girl goodbye I noticed him breathing in her scent, as though storing the fragrance for future remembrance.

No sooner had he closed the door behind the woman when he turned to me and pronounced, with pleasure beaming from his features,

"She is quite something Bunny, no?"

"Yes," I replied – with slightly less enthusiasm.

"Mary is one out of a hundred women I warrant. Or rather she is a hundred women in one," Raffles gaily asserted, perhaps as much to himself as to me.

Chapter Nine

We settled upon going to the Savoy for lunch. "A change is as good as a rest," Raffles argued. Of course our natural conservatism soon scorned this notion of change when we witnessed how busy it was, although (I argued) we were steeped in blood so far that should we wade no more, returning would be as tedious as remaining. And what with the menu looking palatable we decided to take a table.

Lavender drenched dowagers, long-winded briefs, idle aristocrats working on their gout, actresses and mistresses (often one in the same) populated the tables too. All inhuman life was here. Judges dined with senior ministers, proving that the legislative and executive parts of the government are not entirely separate. Brash American tourists screwed up their pates at the meagre sizes of the portions – and the over inflated prices. They would soon be off to Bond St to pick up a fake Old Master, or genuine English heiress. Politicians sat with financiers and industrialists and sold the kind of favours that not even the actresses had the morals, or lack of, to countenance.

I had the scallops – so small and lacking in number as to make it a game almost to locate them in the accompanying green salad – and a tolerable brace of lamb cutlets. Raffles had the salmon and partridge. There wasn't a vintage in the world that would have befitted all of our dishes so we just worked our way through two bottles of a trusted burgundy.

"Now, Bunny, this is as much a business lunch as anything else. Although Fuller's apartment will prove a tough nut to crack, even Troy fell. And we have the wooden horse of myself at the Albany," Raffles remarked, smiling into his wine glass. "My plan is as follows. Fuller will be throwing a drinks party for his City cronies this Friday evening. We must entice our quarry out of his apartment during the afternoon. I will invite him to lunch, at the Savile. It is my guess that he will leave his keys in his overcoat pocket, in which case they will be easy to retrieve in the cloakroom of the club. Whilst Fuller is kept occupied throughout the afternoon I can easily get to the Albany, enter his apartment and get back in time without him suspecting a thing. He will probably only realise that he has been robbed after the drinks party – in which case it will be his guests under suspicion, rather than anyone else."

Raffles here paused as a striking red-headed filly attracted his attention. A hint of desire first coloured his gaze, but then he looked wistful or melancholy even. Was he thinking of Mary Flanagan? The woman disappeared from view however and he continued to elaborate upon his plan.

"Now the question is how will we lure our rabbit out of his hole and keep him occupied for the duration of lunch and beyond?"

As if inspired by the same daemon we replied in unison after pausing in thought for a few moments,

"Fry!"

We both grinned, sumptuously – and even clinked our glasses, toasting ourselves in anticipation of success.

Chapter Ten

Raffles and I often called C.B. Fry 'Charles III', a name that Vanity Fair bestowed upon him in an article earlier on in the decade, in which it listed some of his startling achievements. Whilst not yet twenty-two years of age Fry had earned an Oxford Blue in cricket, football and athletics (as well as being a leading light in the Debating and Literary Societies at Wadham College; people also flocked to his acting debut for the 'hell' of it, in that he caused quite a stir by uttering the aforementioned swear word as part of his role). For many a year Fry also jointly held the world record for the long jump – and should he have taken part I wager that he could have won a medal at the Olympic Games in sprinting and hurdling – and perhaps even the high, as well as long, jump. Fry played rugby at a high level too, being picked to play for Blackheath, the Barbarians and Oxford. A friend of mine had seen him play at rugby – and despite it being one of his lesser sports he still performed well enough to inspire his own chant during games, "Fry! Fly! Try!" Such were his achievements whilst a student at university that he was nicknamed 'Lord Oxford' and the 'Almighty'. Raffles also mentioned to me once how Wadham was deemed of consisting of 'Fry and small fry.' As well as representing England at both football and cricket, Charles Burgess Fry could also talk for England (albeit often on his specialist subject of Charles Burgess Fry) – which is why we both of us thought that Charles III could hold court and distract Fuller during the duration of the robbery. Ideally he would provide a distraction up until the early evening, when the banker's drinks party commenced.

In some ways Fry looked more like Raffles' brother than friend, such was their similar appearance. They shared similar (handsome) features, including eyes which could hold one's aspect as much as Coleridge's Ancient Mariner. Fry's moustache was akin to that of Raffles' also – and they both possessed athletic physiques, although C.B. was perhaps a little taller and broader (his tutors at Wadham had often referred to him as looking like a Greek God, or having a body sculptured by the hands of Praxilites). Their hair was similar, though Raffles parted his hair on the other side, and different tailors still helped produce an overlapping sartorial elegance. Even their batting styles had been compared to one another - although Raffles, through mirroring Ranji's wristy technique, scored more confidently down the leg side in my humble opinion. Fry's driving however was both powerful and accurate – to the point where perhaps he was only rivalled in the art by Trumper and Grace.

Thankfully Fry and Raffles had arranged to speak on the telephone after our lunch that day – and he gladly accepted our invitation to meet at the Savile on Friday. Not wishing to miss the opportunity to be introduced to one of the most celebrated men of the day – and perhaps even collect him like a hat – Fuller leapt at the chance and cancelled a business appointment so as to assent to the invitation. Raffles had fuelled their appetite for the lunch by saying to Fry that Fuller was a fan and keen to meet him – and he had also accordingly mentioned to Fuller that Fry was looking forward to meeting the larger than life financier.

I spent the Thursday working, writing a cliché ridden review of an even greater cliché ridden novel. From smelling her perfume upon his jacket, I surmised that Raffles had spent the day (and perhaps night) with Mary Flanagan. Raffles and I arranged to have supper at the Savile, booking a table for lunch the following day as we did so. I met Raffles at the bar, talking to a young man. I caught the end of their exchange, as my friend handed the chubby-faced youth a glass of champagne, poured from a bottle of Pol Roger that he was working his way through.

"In victory, deserve it. In defeat, need it," Raffles sagely expressed as he passed the glass over.

"Thank you."

"What do you think?"

"I could get used to it," the young man replied, smiling as if he had just tasted the elixir of life. "I must return to my dinner companions now."

And with that the young man trundled upstairs.

"How are you old boy? Would you like a glass?"

"Certainly. We are all set for tomorrow it seems. But tell me –"

"You will be pleased to know that Fry will not be being

accompanied by Beattie."

Beattie was C.B's wife. During her youth she had been a famed beauty, although greater fame had been achieved through her scandalous affair with the married banker Charles Hoare. Hoare had taken Beattie as a mistress whilst she was still in her teens. A court case ensued, in an attempt to prosecute Hoare for his impropriety. Eventually Hoare lived with his mistress and, as well as setting up house together, they founded a naval academy and schooled young boys in seamanship. Their affections waned for each other however. It was all quite sudden but Fry and Beattie met and married each other one summer. Some say that C.B married Beattie for her money and connections – and as a result of her wealth he was able to resign from his teaching position at Charterhouse and play a full season's cricket. Yet Fry was his own man and I warrant he married for love, albeit the woman who walked down the aisle upon their wedding day bore little resemblance to the harridan who he would gladly leave behind in Sussex to visit Raffles for. Beattie was around ten years older than Fry – and he now possessed the better figure and fewer grey hairs compared to his wife. She was as stern and shrewish towards Charles as she was towards her students aboard the Mercury, the vessel on which she taught practical seamanship. I had never known her to laugh – and her natural expression was one of grim severity. A part of her was still perhaps devoted to Hoare – and rumours abounded that Fry's first child was really Hoare's. Beattie was also a devotee of Wagner and subscribed to the philosophy that life is a struggle. Certainly one could say of Fry that he found married life a struggle. She dressed quite mannishly and in many ways, when one had the misfortune to suffer her company, Beattie acted the husband to Fry's wife. She was a singular creature, neither male nor female. My blood could curdle at just the mentioning of her name. Nietzsche once posited, in one of his aphorisms, that "Woman – that was God's second mistake." I could not but smile the other day when Raffles misquoted the philosopher by drily stating, "Beattie – that was God's third mistake." She provided all of the argument that I needed to remain a bachelor.

I sighed with relief upon hearing that Fry would be venturing up to London alone. I then asked Raffles,

"Who was that young chap just at the bar?"

"That was Winston, Randolph Churchill's son."

"Let's hope that the apple falls far from the tree."

"Aye, as far away so as to be in another orchard. But I believe that it will."

Chapter Eleven

I met Fry at the station the following day and we took a hansom to the Savile, having planned to meet Raffles and Fuller at the club, as opposed to the Albany. The day was clear, but the temperature was sufficiently bracing as to make us all put on our overcoats. Fry was also dressed in a navy blue flannel suit, with shoes as polished as his manners. He shook my hand and then his taut body, hewn from bronze almost, embraced my slightly less taut frame. Charles was in good spirits and we shared our latest news and gossip. I asked after Ranji – and out of politeness I asked after Beattie – and we also spoke about possible subjects for Fry's forthcoming column in *the Strand* magazine. Although he could sometimes be a snob and self-obsessed when in the company of strangers, either trying to impress them or living up to his lionised image, I always found C.B. to be warm, earnest and generous when in the company of close friends. We had met through Raffles, but our friendship was now our own. I admired him immensely – who wouldn't? – but just as much for the man that he was off the cricket field than for the immortal he was upon it.

Heads turned and the air rippled with whispers and murmurings as C.B and I entered the club. I could not help but beam and puff out my chest, just to be associated with the 'Almighty'. Even I am not immune to a certain degree of vanity.

Fry and Fuller were introduced to one another. Both were affable and magnanimous towards each other, with both perhaps believing that they were the guest of honour. Yet even Fuller remained slightly tongue-tied, deferent. For C.B. Fry ranked even higher than A.J. Raffles on the Elizabethan chain of being.

Raffles apologised profusely for having to attend to some business during lunch, but he had a drink with us upon our arrival in the bar and promised to re-join us before the end of the afternoon. He gave me a wink and a reassuring smile before finally departing. I gulped down my first glass of chardonnay quicker than normal, out of a mixture of nerves and excitement. Raffles mentioned that he would return immediately on some pre-text should he not be able to find Fuller's keys in his overcoat pocket in the cloakroom – but five minutes had passed and I realised that the job was on. Raffles was now striding down Piccadilly towards the Albany to burgle the man that I was convivially having lunch with.

We decided to have one more drink in the bar before sitting down to lunch. Fry had already played himself in so to speak, in regards to holding court and guiding the conversation. He entertained the table – and a few within earshot of where we were sitting - with the following story (which I must confess that I had heard as many times as C.B. had scored centuries).

"...I was a few minutes late upon joining the selection committee. The moment I entered the door W.G. said, 'Here's Charles. Now, Charles, before you sit down, we want you to answer this question, yes or no. Do you think that Archie Maclaren ought to play in the next Test Match?' Now, Archie Maclaren had in the winter of 1897-98 been the most successful batsman in the team taken to Australia by A.E Stoddart... He had played Jones with great success. He was on top of the Australian bowling as a whole. Our batting had not shown up well during the first Test at Nottingham... so I answered without hesitation, 'Yes, I do.' 'That settles it,' said W.G.; and I sat down at the table. Then, and not until then, did I discover that the question W.G. had asked me meant, 'Shall I, W.G. Grace, resign from the England eleven?' This had never occurred to me. I had thought that it was merely a question of Archie coming in instead of one of the other batsmen... I explained this, and I tried to hedge, but the others had made up their minds that I was to be confronted with a sudden casting vote. So there it was. I who owed my place in the England team to W.G.'s belief in me as a batsman gave the casting vote that ended W.G.'s career of cricket... Of course we all believed he was worth his place as a batsman, but Grace confessed that he could not contribute anything in earnest in the field. He wistfully confessed that 'the ground was too far away from me' to carry on playing Test cricket."

Although we could have waited to be served our drinks I volunteered to go up to the bar. It was whilst waiting at the bar that I casually picked up a newspaper. Noticing Arrows' name at the bottom of an article I decided to read the short piece. But turned into dread within a minute.

'...As the judge pronounced the sentence Edward Salter shook his head, as much in self-pity as disbelief. The wife of the estate agent, his family and friends all similarly shook their heads. It was perhaps the absent figure of Marie Finnigan though who occupied the thoughts of the guilty man. He had described the governess as being slender, pretty – and having long red-hair and freckles. If real, as opposed to being a mere fictional scapegoat for the crimes of Mr Salter, then we can also perhaps recognise Miss Finnigan by her newly acquired jewels – or from the smile on her face, at having committed the perfect crime'

One did not need to be Sherlock Holmes to deduce that Marie Finnigan was also Mary Flanagan – but yet I felt the urge to rush to Raffles, like Watson to Holmes's side, and deliver this news. I did not know how this information would impact upon my friend – I just knew that it would. My lunch companions barely gave me a second thought as I explained how I needed to pass on some papers to Raffles for his business meeting. I was forgiven immediately – and perhaps even forgotten shortly after that – as I absented myself too from lunch.

Chapter Twelve

With little thought for the spectacle that I was doubtless making, I sprinted and weaved my way out of St James' and along Piccadilly. I slowed to a walk and tried to catch my breath and regain my composure however as I got to the Albany and greeted the doorman, Clarence. Once out of his sight I proceeded to bound up the stairs. As I reached the top landing I saw Raffles enter Fuller's apartment. I reached him and entered the apartment too. We stood in the hallway. Concern and bafflement lined his usually unperturbed features. I clasped my hand on my friend's shoulder, partly to steady myself and partly to pull him back from some imagined precipice.

"Bunny, what's wrong?"

I could but pant like a dog in reply. I need not have spoken her name however as I looked up to find Mary Flanagan or Marie Finnigan – or whoever the she-devil was – standing behind Raffles with a gun in her hand. The last time that Raffles had heard the unmistakable sound of a gun being cocked he had rolled his eyes in annoyance, or tedium even. This time he merely closed his eyes and half smiled, in either wonderment or expectation (I could not rightly discern which in the half light).

"Hello Mary," Raffles uttered, without even turning around to see who was pointing the gun at him.

"How did you know it was me? Did you recognise my perfume?" she replied.

"No, although I did spend some time with a perfumer at Fortnum and Mason the other day, in order to discover the fragrance that you wear. As I suspected it is not entirely affordable on a maid's salary. I also had an acquaintance of mine in Limehouse look in to the provenance of you and your family living in Bermondsey. Things add up."

"I can thankfully afford more expensive perfume – and lodgings for my family – these days. We did once live there however – and I did once work as a maid and train to be a nurse if it's any consolation."

"It is, believe it or not. When did you suspect me of having a second career?" Raffles replied. He still kept his back to the woman, as though to witness her holding a gun to him would sadden him too much.

"The night of the party. Firstly, Bunny, you are sweet – but you are a better professional writer than you are an amateur cracksman. I could not help but notice you clumsily case the apartment. Also, when you spoke to me that evening Raffles I realised that you asked the same questions that I would, in regards to gathering information about a prospective job. At first I did not notice however, as it seems you took a genuine interest in Miss Mary Flanagan and liked her. I appreciated that – and I took a genuine interest and like in you as a result. Having stirred my curiosity I went to the library and, instead of reading Ruskin and Milton, I read various sports reports of you playing cricket around the country. I cross referenced them with a number of crime reports of high profile thefts in the same areas at a similar time and it seems there was a correlation. As you say, things add up."

If seeing a gun pointed in my direction did not chill my blood, her cold and callous demeanour could have done the job just as well. Not many women can be deemed pretty when they scowl. Even more so than Raffles there was a fundamental duality to this young woman's existence. She did not consider that she had to live by the rules – and morality – that others lived by.

"And would I have become a job as well?"

"Yes. Although I would have left you with your cricket bats – and jemmy. I would not have wished to take away your livelihood. As for Rupert Robert Fuller, I have no qualms about taking everything from him. He has taken far more from others over the years. His banks have foreclosed on thousands of families like mine. He has caused more wanton destruction to people's livelihood than any war. Now I must ask you to do me the professional courtesy of leaving. I have work to do. After all you must concede that I got here first. And I would much rather commit larceny than murder."

"I cannot allow you to take everything," Raffles replied, this time with a seriousness – rather than playfulness – in his voice.

"And why is that? Do you think that you are entitled to a share?"

"No. My plan was to but partially rob Fuller. I did not want him noticing until after his party this evening, so as to heap suspicion upon his guests. If he notices upon coming back this afternoon then the spotlight will fall upon me – and also now Bunny. And I cannot allow that."

"You are in no position to allow or disallow anything. I have shot a man before, who tried to take advantage of me. I would also gladly shoot Fuller, should he be here now. And how far removed are you from the likes of him? You are from the same over-indulged and over-privileged background. You are from his class," she scornfully exclaimed, tightening her hand around the handle of the gun as she did so.

"I like to think that I am in a class of my own. Please lower the gun. What we have shared over the past few days has been more than just business – and pleasure – for you." Raffles turned around and gazed at the woman in a conciliatory rather than challenging fashion.

"Ha, are you trying to make me laugh? What makes you think that has been the case?"

"Because it has meant more than just business or pleasure for me."

Raffles stepped towards the woman, but she raised her gun level with his chest as he did so. I was like a limpet against the wall behind him. Fear partly affixed me there, but also the stance gave me a better view of what was happening. Undaunted he took another step. Her eyes widened in shock perhaps more than trepidation.

"Raffles, don't!" she warned, her finger twitching within the trigger guard.

Again he took a step towards her. I was reminded of the scene of when I had stood in Raffles' apartment, on the brink of ruination, and I had placed a gun to my temple and threatened to pull the trigger. Neither fear nor horror resided in his aspect then; nor did they now, as the increasingly desperate woman pointed the gun at him. I was a mere fool and coward though, possessing neither the fire – nor ice – which coursed through this villainess' veins. If she fired now she could not fail to hit him.

"Don't, please. I don't want to shoot you."

"I know, I'd rather you didn't shoot me either. Mary Flanagan would not want to wish me injury as well, as much as I would welcome her nursing me back to health. She could help nurse you back to health, too."

When Raffles stepped forward this time the woman took half a step back.

"I have injured kinder men than you who have stood in my way. And Mary Flanagan is but an act. Do not mistake her for me. You more than anyone know how people can just play a part, Raffles."

"We both like Mary Flanagan and you enjoy the role too much to want it to remain wholly an act I believe. She's too much a part of you, even if she seems a mere ghost in your past. She would not want to kill a friend over some jewellery and money. She knows that "there is no wealth but life". Perhaps the world hurt you and you want to hurt it back. But do not let people who care about you get caught in the crossfire."

Again Raffles walked forward and again the woman took half

a step back. The gun was trembling a little in her hand and I was wary that it could go off accidentally.

"Is this the way that you plead for your life?" she issued.

"No, this is the way that I am pleading for yours."

Chapter Thirteen

No sooner did Raffles carefully take the gun out of her hands than she fell into his arms. I do not know how long I had been holding my breath for but at that moment I finally breathed out. I also do not know how long Raffles just held the young woman for, her head buried in his chest. But I do know the following: Tears stained his shirt-front afterwards. We also all proceeded to partially rob Fuller – and as Raffles predicted the investigation the next day was centred upon the guests at the party that evening. As a coda to the fate of Rupert Robert Fuller he was shortly afterwards investigated for tax evasion and fraud. It seems that a couple of incriminating accounts and documents had been removed from his safe and sent to the relevant authorities. Despite all of Fuller's friends in high places, the prosecuting civil servants served the Crown rather than the ruling political party of the day and justice prevailed.

Raffles offered our entire haul to the woman who had, not an hour beforehand, threatened to shoot him. She insisted that we take half of the spoils however.

"Allow me one point of principle, as a thief," she playfully remarked.

"As long as you realise that any profit will continue to fund my over-indulged and over-privileged lifestyle," he equally playfully replied. She laughed, squeezed him on the hand and sweetly kissed his cheek.

Raffles and I made our way back to the Savile. Neither of us appeared to be missed by our two lunch guests. We walked in with Fuller – and half of those at the club – captivated by Fry giving a demonstration of the perfect on drive (having commandeered a member's walking stick to use as a substitute for a bat). Raffles made a gift of a pair of gold cufflinks as a present to our friend – and unwitting decoy – at the close of the day.

"Heavens, what are these for?" C.B asked, touched and lost a little for words (for once).

"No reason. They are just a thank you present for you being yourself old chap," Raffles replied, fraternally patting him on the back as he boarded the train back to Sussex.

Raffles had arranged to have lunch with his gentlewoman thief the following day but – as I suspect that he suspected – she did not show. She had left a note for the restaurant to give to him however, by way of an apology and explanation.

Dear Raffles,

Please forgive my absence. I do not want you to think I have lost my pluck, but I do not feel comfortable and confident to wholly come out of the shadows just yet. Let us both just feast upon the memories and fond times we shared, rather than think about any possible future that we may have together. We both know that we could never be a conventional couple. Please pass on my regards to Bunny. I could perhaps add that you should continue to look out for him – but more so I would like you to tell Bunny that he should continue to look out for you. P.S You can tell him shortly as I have invited him to lunch here for 2.30. And lunch is on me by way of a thank you, for everything. Your friend, Mary.'

The note was also accompanied by a copy of *Paradise Regained & Samson Agonistes*, by Milton. The inscription inside read, *'What good is strength without double the wisdom.'*

I wish I could say whether the scented paper was signed *'Mary'* because of a symbolic change enwrought by Raffles in the young woman's heart – but it could have just as easily been her real name. As to the fate of Marie Finnigan however, I read a follow-up article by Arrows a week later reporting how a woman of her description had left a parcel, as well as a letter, for the investigating officer of the Salter case at the police station. Within a day Edward Salter was released from Newgate and back with his wife – and her jewels – at his home in Barnes.

Raffles and I had a long lunch, in Mary's absence. She had ordered three bottles of Pol Roger for us, among other things. It was quite late when we got back to the Albany, but we shared a glass of port together and I asked,

"Will you be sad not to see her again? In some ways you were made for each other, no?"

"Perhaps she would always be too good for me, or I too good for her. But that could just be the drink talking, old chap. As to whether I will be sad not to see Mary again, I thankfully possess other griefs that can cast such sadness into the darkness," Raffles philosophically – or mournfully – replied whilst lighting a new candle upon his desk, from the stump of the old.

RAFFLES:

A PERFECT WICKET

Chapter One

Grey clouds smeared themselves across the sky. Rain freckled the windows. Raffles' mood was as grim as the weather. Not two weeks had passed since our encounter with, for want of knowing her real name, Mary Flanagan. The details of our week planning and robbing Rupert Robert Fuller – and the course of Raffles' affair with the remarkable Miss Flanagan – can be found in Raffles: Bowled Over. Perhaps Raffles was listless from missing her. For many a job – and affair – would pale in comparison to the events of that week. Yet I had seen him sink into such drear moods before, without the aid of a woman or a lack of adventure, so I wasn't altogether convinced by my theory.

It was two o'clock. I called upon my friend at the Albany after a lunch with Thomas 'Arrows' Fletcher, a journalist chum of mine. An unshaven Raffles welcomed me in and poured me a gin and tonic, but he soon sat wordlessly in his armchair, still in his dressing gown – pensively staring either out of the window or upon the solitary candle which burned upon his desk before the windowpane. His expression reminded me of a couplet composed by Byron who, as much perhaps from sympathy as due to the fact that the poet once resided in the Albany too, Raffles called his 'neighbour'.

'Full many a stoic eye and aspect stern
Mask hearts where grief has little left to learn.'

The dregs of a whisky and soda-water sat upon a table next to him, as did an ashtray which contained a veritable pyramid of cigarette butts. We sat in silence for what may have been half an hour or so, during which Raffles smoked another three Sullivans. I kept telling myself that the next cigarette butt laid upon the pile would cause the entire edifice to collapse, but Raffles possessed (or was possessed by) either the luck or skill of the devil. After finishing off another whisky and soda-water, consisting of a nigh on equal measure of both, Raffles turned to me. Realising perhaps how forlorn I was, from witnessing my usually bright companion enmeshed in a gloom, he tried to smile – but the feeble effort failed to convince either of us.

"My apologies, Bunny. I am not myself today – or rather I am myself today. I do not know. How weary, stale, flat and unprofitable seem to me all the uses of this world, so to speak." Again, he attempted to smile but his heart wasn't in it. Indeed his faltering smile made him seem all the more melancholy or pained.

"What's wrong, old chap? Are you in need of a doctor?"

"No. I warrant that I am more in need of some sport. Rather than being ill – or worse than being ill – I am bored. Kierkegaard argued that 'boredom is the root of all evil.' Tolstoy posited that boredom is the 'desire for desires.' Oh, I can but fruitlessly wax upon my malady my friend, but can you help deliver a cure?"

There was a mixture of satire as well as sincerity in his tone. I was here about to suggest an evening at the casino but I knew only too well the kind of sport that Raffles craved. It involved breaking into a house, rather than breaking the bank at the casino.

"Well I'm not sure that I can help deliver a cure to your boredom, but I can deliver your mail. I picked it up in the lobby," I replied whilst retrieving two letters from my pocket and passing them to my friend.

The first piece of mail – some form of an overdue bill I dare say – duly increased rather than assuaged his sense of tedium and frustration. Raffles rolled his eyes, before screwing up the letter and envelope and tossing them onto the fire. Yet he knit his brow with intrigue rather than vexation upon reading the second piece of correspondence. Within the space of thirty seconds the twinkle returned to my good friend's eye, like the sun breaking through thick clouds. A divinity and devilry returned to his expression. He grinned and enthusiastically clasped me by the arm.

"By God Bunny, you have delivered both the mail and the cure. The game's afoot!"

Chapter Two

A light, autonomous of the flames from the fireplace, danced in Raffles' eyes as he poured me another gin and tonic and handed me the letter.

'*Dear Raffles,*

I hope that you are well. You will be pleased to know that the hat you kindly bought me in Bond St last week has indeed been turning heads in Truro. A few comments have been complimentary, but I have much rather enjoyed the looks of disdain and disapproval that I have been generating, from priggish duffers and prudish old women alike, by wearing my 'shockingly modern bonnet.' The local paper may well even run a story about my scandalous behaviour, such is the paucity of other things happening, or rather not happening, in town.

As you can see, I have enclosed an invite to a party which is taking place this weekend. I do hope that you will be free to attend as my guest. You will be welcome to stay for the weekend. Bunny will be welcome, too. I first became acquainted with Lord Rosebery through being introduced to him at the races. He was initially curious about me due to my surname I suspect, even though we are not related. But we have corresponded since and I count

him as a good friend – and one of the most remarkable men in England.
I know that he would be interested in meeting you. You are both lively
conversationalists, lovers of sport – contrarians and introverts.

Lucy.'

'Lucy' was Lucy Rosebery, a delightful and stimulating young
woman (who must have been no younger than twenty and no
older than twenty-five). Raffles had first met her whilst playing
cricket in Truro. When he had mentioned Miss Rosebery upon
returning to London he could barely contain his fondness and
admiration for her, but time – or Mary Flanagan – had cooled
his ardour. Raffles had been but perfunctorily charming when
Lucy had visited him a week ago, suspending his black mood
out of politeness rather than inspiration. He took her for lunch
and showered her with gifts, rather than genuine attention and
affection, in Bond St afterwards. Unbeknownst to Lucy, Raffles
proceeded to spend the evening with her cousin, Margaret, who
was also in town for the week. Although I could not help but
disapprove of my friend's caddish behaviour it did afford me the
opportunity to spend an agreeable evening with Miss Rosebery
at the theatre. I tried to admonish him again the following day
however.

"Your loss was my gain," I argued (my attempts at instilling a
sense of shame in Raffles appeared to have little or no effect, at
best).

"I agree, Bunny. You can be assured that I will not be seeing
Margaret again in favour of Lucy. I warrant that all that lies

between her ears – pretty ears though they may be – are pictures of bridal gowns and flower arrangements. Suffice to say I would rather attend a funeral service, my own even, to that of a marriage service involving myself. Also, she snores in bed."

I coloured upon hearing this revealing comment. Whether I admired, disapproved or envied Raffles in regards to his efficient seduction of the somewhat coquettish Margaret my immediate thoughts were for her cousin.

"You have not – I mean with Lucy, also –"

"No, Margaret is much more the kissing cousin so to speak out of the two. I get the impression that our virtuous young suffragette keeps the key to her heart inside the same locket which houses the key to her chastity belt. There was a time when I would have considered breaking into such a locket a piece of good sport. But I would much rather break into something nowadays that I can steal and fence, rather than steal and just write poetry about."

I was more than a tad upset at Raffles for having spoken in such an unbecoming way about Miss Rosebery, who I must confess had made quite a favourable impression on me the evening before. But at least Raffles' witticisms brought a smile back to his face and lessened his melancholy humour, however briefly.

Lord Rosebery needs no introduction of course. He is the man who famously set himself the three ambitions of marrying an heiress, winning the Derby and becoming Prime Minster – of which he managed all three before the age of fifty.

Raffles tipped the contents of his ashtray into the fire, which momentarily choked the flames, and downed another whisky and soda, slamming the tumbler back on the table and licking his lips as he did so.

"This job could prove to be my Sistine Chapel, Aeneid or Parsifal."

I was here tempted to say that it could also prove to be his Waterloo, with Raffles playing the part of Napoleon, but I did not wish to dampen my friend's positive mood. He was soaring into the sun again. I already knew that I would cancel whatever was in my diary to attend the party.

"I will get dressed and we will venture out. We should treat ourselves to a new suit or two in light of the party Bunny, with specially designed deep pockets," he playfully remarked (albeit I must confess that I did not know whether his comment was wholly in jest or not).

"Alas, my current shallow pockets are all but empty," I replied. The Baccarat tables had been as amenable to me as the weather that week.

"Fret not, old chap. Come with me. I will help fill both your pockets and your wardrobe."

Chapter Three

As Raffles shaved and dressed I asked Clarence, the ever-obliging doorman at the Albany, to arrange for a cab to take us to the King's Rd. As we headed west, the rain drumming upon the canopy of the hansom, Raffles spoke enthusiastically – and fondly even – about the man he was intending to rob.

"Did you know that he was thrown out of Oxford? Rosebery purchased a racehorse, which was against college rules. He was granted the choice to either keep the racehorse or leave the college. Earlier on in the year the college had predicted that Rosebery would attain a first. They were not sharp enough to predict his reply however. Now there's pluck, Bunny... He has been as equally profligate as generous with his fortune, I understand... Yet I am not of that insipid, Eton-hating set who despise – as much as they envy – wealth and privilege. Indeed I would rather we have more politicians of Rosebery's ilk who go into office with money, as opposed to this ever increasing political class we have now who go in to office to make money..."

Thankfully it was but a short walk from where we disembarked upon the King's Rd to the small flat which served as Raffles' second home, for his double-life as an amateur cracksman. The apartment housed various accoutrements to his trade, as well as a number of changes of clothes (including a police constable's uniform even). The flat was also home to a small safe, hidden behind an accomplished copy of a Caspar David Friedrich landscape (or it was entirely possible, knowing Raffles, that the painting was the original). Once in the apartment Raffles went to the safe and removed a diamond studded tiepin and a couple of other pieces of jewellery, which I recognised as spoils from the Rupert Robert Fuller robbery.

"I have been saving these for a rainy day," Raffles remarked, his aspect twinkling as much as the tiepin. "It's never a good idea to sell all the loot in one go Bunny, so I kept these beauties back. As ever half the take will be yours. Here, put these on – and these. I want you to accompany me to Limehouse, where we'll offload them to a fence I know."

Raffles here handed me some bedraggled overalls from his wardrobe, made from a material that was coarser than the docker's language that had originally possessed the ill-styled garments. I was also presented with a pair of ill-fitting black boots which looked like they had last been polished when Rosebery had been Prime Minister half a decade ago.

Raffles donned similar clothes and besmirched both of our faces a little. Although we would look out of place somewhat in Chelsea, we would doubtless fit right in around Limehouse. He tucked a small cosh in his inside pocket and I gulped as he tossed me a similar baton.

"Fail to prepare, prepare to fail," Raffles exclaimed, with a warped sense of adventure rather than gravity in his expression.

Suffice to say that if my boots had not been so steel-capped, I would have here verily kicked myself – for my decision not to have that second bottle with Arrows at lunch and so avoid this potentially perilous escapade with Raffles.

Chapter Four

This was the first time that Raffles had invited me to accompany him to Limehouse, or any of his other haunts in the East End or south of the river where he sold on the fruits of our labour. Perhaps he thought he was satisfying my curiosity – or equally it may have been he wanted to amuse himself by watching me deal with such an alien environment. In little or no time at all I realised however that I would be happy for this to be the last time that Raffles invited me to accompany him.

Narrow streets and tall, ugly buildings blocked out what little sunlight there was seeping through the grey clouds. The pavements were slick with grime – and steaming puddings of dung populated the roads. People (dock workers, charwomen, vagrants, costermongers, ruffians) shouted rather than spoke to each other in language far more colourful than the sky above. Noxious fumes wafted along the noxious looking Thames and permeated every nook and cranny. I would have perhaps fainted, if not for the fear of falling into the dung and grime. I couldn't help but turn my nose up at the undesirables – and unsmellables – who jostled along the street with me. Yet I was also conscious of not looking anyone in the eye. It was not just the rapidly forming blister upon my left heel which made me look uncomfortable I warrant.

Raffles however seemed to be both enjoying playing his part and watching me squirm playing mine. As soon as he had put on his costume his manner had altered dramatically – and realistically. His Cockney was as proficient as his Latin – and Raffles appeared as at ease with the scene and etiquette of Limehouse as he was with Piccadilly. He was still devilishly handsome even in disguise though – and the young barmaid duly smiled and blushed as he doffed his cap to her, made a joke and ordered a couple of drinks in the public house he steered me into.

"Now I want you to keep your eyes open and mouth shut, Bunny. Nod, shrug or shake your head should any of our fellow patrons engage with you," Raffles whispered whilst leading me into a quiet crevice of the tavern.

The establishment reeked of gin and beer – and the waste product the body releases after drinking the aforementioned. Customers either bellowed all manner of things to each other or murmured in corners. The language was often as filthy as the tankards we drank out of. Most of the men – and a couple of the women, too – had beards and were dressed not dissimilarly to myself. Many of them turned their heads when they heard the door creak open, perhaps fearing that their employers, or worse wives, might enter and scold them.

"I'm here to see the wizened old gent in the corner," Raffles quietly remarked, subtly nodding his head in the direction of the fence.

Tufts of wiry grey hair sprouted out from beneath a battered brown trilby hat. His eyes nervously flitted around the room and his hands remained in constant motion – fingering his beard, handling his watch, picking crumbs and fluff from his woollen jacket.

"His name is Spokes. He's half Jewish and half Irish Catholic, but wholly dedicated to Mammon. Like many in his profession he will plead poverty but when finished for the day, old Spokes will leave Limehouse to go home to a three-storey house in Hampstead. A cook and maid will serve as staff then, as opposed to the two minders who are sat behind him at present. I once spotted him in Jermyn St, buying a suit of slightly finer quality to that which he is wearing now. Spokes is also a moneylender – and Shylock himself would blanch at the rates of interest he charges. In short, I'd rather deal with the crafty old Fagan than most of his brethren, but I trust him about as much as a priest or trade union leader."

I tried my best not to wince, or wretch, upon taking a swig of beer (in as natural a manner as I could muster – consciously keeping my little finger tightly clasped around the mug, instead of pointing to the ceiling). Raffles caught Spokes' eye and the fence gave him the nod to come over to his corner, but both suddenly desisted upon seeing two other rogues approach the table. The first man, who sat down opposite to the fence, was stocky and dressed like a dandy. He was middle-aged, but his piratical good looks still gave him a virile air. Striking green eyes shone out beneath his cap and surveyed, or pierced, the room in one scoping glance. Even Spokes' minders averted their gaze. The second rogue was a bear of a man, with a bull neck and a flat, porcine face. Scars lined his shaven head as if it were an ordnance survey map. He was proof enough of Mr Darwin's controversial theory than man is descended from the ape.

"We are now in the presence of royalty, Bunny. That man sitting down with Spokes is none other than Jack Shanks. He's taken more jewellery, cash, paintings, thoroughbred horses – and lives – than any other player in the game. Aye, I am a gentleman to his player. I am an amateur. Shanks is a professional thief. He robs through both force and guile, arming himself with either a clever disguise or shotgun – or both. He once even broke in to the Old Bailey, dressed as a barrister, and stole evidence that would have convicted a member of his gang.. Shanks is feared and loved in equal measure," Raffles reported, partly in awe and partly in wariness.

I must confess that I felt more fear than love at this point for this master rogue – and I even downed a few mouthfuls of beer in an attempt to steady my nerves. I also felt somewhat deficient in that whereas Shanks had brought along a bulldog to watch his back, Raffles merely possessed a Bunny.

Chapter Five

Neither Raffles nor I overheard their exchange at the table, albeit little seemed to be said. Shanks shook his head a couple of times, before finally accepting the fence's improved offer for the contents of the bag that he had brought in with him. Spokes then shook his head and shrugged, after paying over the money, as if to convey that he'd not had the better of the deal and he would barely make a profit when selling the items on.

With little fanfare Jack Shanks then went up to the bar and quietly spoke to the barmaid,

"A drink for everyone Daisy – and two for yourself. I'll square things up tonight."

"Are you not stayin' for a few?"

"No. But don't worry darlin', I'll be back to steal a kiss off you by closin' time. Before that though I've got to steal somethin' less valuable," Shanks charmingly replied.

He stayed not for a beer himself, nor did it seem that he desired the gratitude or acclaim of the bar for buying everyone a drink. He stopped only to take in Raffles, who was standing between the edge of the bar and the door. The strangeness, or irony, of the scene is branded upon my mind even now. The arch-criminal Jack Shanks was dressed somewhat like a gentleman and tried to fashion himself so, whilst Raffles, the true gentleman, was dressed like a common criminal and was trying to fashion himself as such. The two men just merely stared at each other, with neither antagonism nor warmth. Shanks appeared to be sizing the stranger up, as if trying to place him – or trying to discern if he looked out of place. I subtly wiped my sweaty palm upon my trousers, believing that I might soon need to take a firm grip upon my cudgel.

"Do I know you, fella? You look familiar."

"I've been around. But I'm just passin' through," Raffles answered, whilst shrugging.

"That's it, you're the spit of that cricketer. What's 'is name?" he said, turning in vain to his witless – but brutal – minder for the answer.

I here had a vision of the entire edifice of Raffles' existence collapsing, or being tossed into the fire. Society would shun him as swiftly as the police would shackle him. He would need the luck of the devil now to perhaps escape with his life, let alone his reputation intact. Yet still Raffles betrayed not a flicker of distress – appearing bemused, or amused, by the conversation. My heart was racing however, in preparation perhaps for my legs to race away too. My hand reached towards my inside pocket and fingered the tip of the short wooden baton.

"That's it, you look like that gent C.B. Fry. A crackin' batsman. I saw 'im, or you rather (he here laughed a little at his own joke), at Lord's in May."

"I only wish I were 'im – and had 'is money. Although 'aving seen a picture of his wife in the paper, 'e can keep 'er," Raffles replied in good humour.

Shanks grinned at the joke, although his green eyes remained unsmiling. Aye, I remember there being something dead, or murderous, about those eyes. The clock upon the wall here chimed, reminding the legendary cracksman that he was running late. Time is the ultimate thief I guess, for not even Pinkerton or Sherlock Holmes can recover what it spirits away.

The rogue doffed his cap to Raffles, and Raffles replied in kind, before he departed. The sweat upon my brow had cut streaks through the blacking upon my face. I blew air out from my cheeks and shook my head, marvelling at my friend's regal insouciance.

"By Jove, that was close," I whispered, still recovering from our reprieve.

"My dear Bunny, I have stared down a snarling Ernie Jones and F.R. Spofforth, on pitches with the bounce as uneven as a fishwife's temper. I'll be damned if I'll lose my sangfroid to Jack Shanks. To reiterate. Money lost – little lost. Honour lost – much lost. Pluck lost – all lost. Suffice to say though that this is one C.B. Fry anecdote that won't be recounted by Charles at the Savile."

Chapter Six

Unfortunately it seems that Raffles neither possessed the desired valuables nor the intimidating authority of Jack Shanks when dealing with the wily fence. It was Raffles' turn to shrug his shoulders and shake his head as we returned to the King's Rd and he expressed his slight disappointment at the amount that our haul had raised.

"Still, what goes around comes around. Especially with Spokes."

After changing back into our slightly more well cut clothes we ventured back to Piccadilly, stopping off at the Cafe Royal to have supper.

"The women who dine there are as fine as the wine and the new chef is first rate. You should try the river crab as a first course. Dinner will be on me old chap, or rather Rupert Robert Fuller."

We were glad of our choice of restaurant however before even the first sip of the Chablis passed our lips, for as we were entering we bumped into a merry Ranji, who was leaving the establishment. Raffles considered K.S. Ranjitsinhji, 'the Indian Prince', to be the greatest batsman of the age – and having bowled against and batted with many of Ranji's rivals Raffles was qualified to know. "The pain of him scoring runs off you all around the wicket is offset by the aesthetic pleasure of watching him do so... I am reminded of a quote by Schopenhauer Bunny, in trying to encapsulate Ranji's superiority in executing strokes and finding angles that mere mortals cannot imagine, let alone attempt. 'Talent hits a target that no one else can hit; Genius hits a target no one else can see.'" Akin to Raffles, Ranji was one of the most generous men I have ever known – and partly as a result of this he was also one of the most debt-ridden. Aye, as much as one could admire Ranji as a batsman, the likes of Raffles and his great batting partner C.B. Fry loved him more as a friend.

Ranji was wearing one of his famous silk shirts beneath his jacket. A genial grin shone out from beneath his ever smartly trimmed moustache as he clasped our hands – before embracing our entire bodies.

"Bunny, I hope you are well. You must come down to Sussex soon, if only to collect a fountain pen that I recently purchased for you. It may not be as mighty as the sword, but it is fine nevertheless. Can I not tempt you both to join me for some drinks? I am out with some old bacchants from Cambridge."

"Forgive us Ranji, but if I don't have something to eat my stomach, along with Bunny, may grumble so much as to wake the neighbours. Another time, though."

"Yes, I must speak with you soon my dear friend," Ranji replied, his tone now more earnest than fraternal. "I could use your advice – and perhaps help. Many a time you've pulled me out of a hole when batting with me. I may now have need of your assistance off the field."

"I am away this weekend, but otherwise you can have a blank cheque in regards to my time and assistance old chap," Raffles warmly responded, disconcerted a little from sensing the anxiety in Ranji's usually relaxed manner.

"Thank you, thank you."

Ranji was then summoned by his brace of companions who had hailed down a hansom cab – and we bid him a good night. Raffles and I proceeded to have dinner. In order to wash the taste of the public house's swill out of my mouth from earlier I had the river crab followed by the poisson in a garlic sauce. A bottle of Chateau Lafite expunged all memory of the wretched establishment from my palate. Raffles was in good spirits throughout the evening and spoke in an animated fashion about all manner of things, though as we had a glass of port back at the Albany he soon relayed the true inspiration behind his buoyant mood.

"The spoils from The Durdans may put us both in clover until the summer Bunny, or beyond. By God, it could indeed be rich pickings this weekend. God or the Devil has put this opportunity in our lap, old chap. We must make hay. It's a perfect wicket!" Raffles exclaimed, his eyes gleaming as brightly as the banquet of loot he was sumptuously imagining.

Chapter Seven

We left for The Durdans, Rosebery's house in Epsom, on the Friday. A lacquer of frost coated every oak, hedgerow and blade of grass as we journeyed out of London and into Surrey on the train. The midday sun soon melted the frost however to leave the landscape lush and glistening like a recently painted picture. Clouds ambled overhead akin to the sheep ambling across the fields. Robins, thrushes and starlings hopped from branch to branch upon skeletal trees in a haze of colour and steam. I caught up on some reading, whilst Raffles caught up on some sleep during the train journey, tipping his hat over his eyes and ignoring his companion – who was eager for discussing the plan for the weekend ahead.

"You have missed some glorious countryside whilst sleeping," I posited when Raffles finally woke up. "It's as if God sub-contracted out the shaping of the landscape to Capability Brown. Nature has been at her most beautiful and benign."

"Hmm, what a book a devil's chaplain might write on the clumsy, wasteful, blundering, low, and horribly cruel work of nature," Raffles replied, quoting Charles Darwin – raising his hat to reveal a raised eyebrow too. "But ignore my cynicism, Bunny. I should be rapped across the knuckles with a volume of Rousseau – and a copy of Virgil should be opened and then slammed shut, with my nose in between its pages. My apologies for having napped during our journey, but I thought it wise to catch up on some sleep now as I plan to be awake during the dead of night this weekend."

A handsome cab collected us from the station and took us to The Durdans.

A buttery light washed over the sloping greenery and manicured shrubbery of the charming estate. Woodpigeons darted overheard, as if practising their manoeuvres for when the shooting season would disturb their idyllic life. The house was large, but still homely rather than grand. Horses whinnied in the nearby stable complex. I heard Rosebery call The Durdans his 'beloved nest' that evening – and I could immediately see why.

Lucy rushed out to greet us upon our arrival. She wore a fetching cream and red dress, which both flowed and yet also showed off her comely figure. She eagerly clasped Raffles by the hands and almost squealed with delight. She seemed glad to see me also – and mentioned how much she had enjoyed reading my recent humorous piece about Salisbury in *The Strand Magazine*. Yet she soon turned her attention back to Raffles, Hyperion to my satirist.

"Would you like me to take you on a tour of the grounds? You may want to stretch your legs after sitting down for so long," Lucy exclaimed. I was unsure whether the invitation extended to myself and I fear I may have looked momentarily bereft somewhat.

"Forgive me Lucy, but could we possibly postpone our walk? I hate to be such a bore, as practised as I am at it, but I would like nothing more now than a nap. I was up late last night and I did not get the chance to sleep upon the train. But I'm sure that Bunny would like to accompany you and see the estate. He loves nothing more than to be immersed in the bower and wilds of nature, providing that a roaring fire and gin and tonic remain within a one mile radius."

I grinned and shook my head, but less so at his witticism than at his stratagem to take a tour around the house, as opposed to its grounds. He had employed the ruse before of wishing to sleep, whilst prowling around unnoticed. What need had I of discussing his plans for the weekend? I already knew them.

Chapter Eight

We were shown up to our rooms but I quickly came back down to accompany Lucy for our turn around the grounds. Although at first she was disappointed at not having Raffles accompany her she soon realised I was the next best thing in that she could talk to me about her would-be suitor. She initially showed me around the stables, where I must confess I but politely feigned interest. The card tables had long consumed any interest – or funds – I might had have in the turf.

"Do you ride, Bunny?"

"No. And the equine community are fine with that fact too, I dare say. I try to avoid both horses – and soapboxes – due to my unfailing ability to fall off them both."

She here laughed. Her laugh was worth a hundred of her smiles – and her smile was priceless.

"I fear that I'm too addicted to climbing upon both, particularly the latter. I know that Raffles may sometimes scoff at my involvement with the cause of women's suffrage, but it is terribly important to me. I hope you understand, Bunny."

Such was the earnest and endearing look that Lucy here gave

me that I would have been willing to sign up there and then to the prattling movement if it meant that she would have believed me in understanding. I was however perhaps ambivalent at best towards the cause. Not only was there a certain amount of conceit and hypocrisy in their campaigning for only some women – those of a certain class – to merit the vote but I was also not without some sympathy for the following comments, made by my journalist friend Thomas Fletcher at lunch that week.

"Women now have access to alcohol, cigarettes and the wonderfully liberating bicycle. They can own property, file for divorce – and dress and shoe sales seem more frequent than ever. The issue of whether they are awarded the vote or not will have less bearing on their levels of contentment than any of the aforementioned, I warrant. God help anyone who would look to a politician to improve their lot."

As ever, Arrows hit the mark.

After touring the stables, in which the horses were tended upon with more care and expense than any patron of Boodles or the Athenaeum even, Lucy proceeded to veer off the paths and we walked upon the undulating parkland which surrounded the house. I could not help but stare – and blush a little – as Lucy lifted up her skirts to reveal her attractive, gleaming calves when the grass grew long or ground grew muddy. She soon trod over old ground however and quizzed me about Raffles. We ended our walk by sitting upon a bench in a pretty arbour close to the house. Trellis work, entwined with myrtle, and apple trees hung overhead. A small pond and a statue of Cupid – albeit his bow was broken – stood in the middle of the garden. Mint and thyme tickled my nostrils and a pair of jays twittered in the background, either flirting or bickering.

"You were at school with him, were you not? Tell me, what was Raffles like in his youth?"

"In many ways he was exactly like he is now, only shorter. Yet for many years, after school, I could not tell you a thing about his history. Perhaps I would have seen him more if I had been a follower of cricket. I heard a rumour once that he was engaged."

"And do you know if he is seeing anyone now? Do you think he will ever marry? When I hint at such questions he deflects things, as if I were bowling him some sort of Yorkie of Googling."

I neither corrected her cricket terminology, nor answered her questions.

"Mama and Papa are becoming less subtle in their hints that I should wed soon. Portia had less prospective suitors visit her than I have had of late. But I do not want to marry someone I do not love and esteem. Marriage should be a meeting of two hearts and minds, not some financial equation or social commandment. It's not as though I will only marry a Mister Knightley or Mister Darcy, I just do not want to marry a Mister Collins or Wickham."

It was not wholly the thought of marrying a Wickham which made Lucy here shiver. Dusk was upon us and the temperature dropped as much as my spirits, upon envisioning the scenario of Raffles breaking her heart.

"Here, take my jacket."

"No, I will be fine."

"Lucy, don't be silly. You may want the vote, but what you need now is a jacket. I'm being firm for once. If I had a soapbox to hand I may even determine to stand on it over the issue."

She smiled that smile that made me smile. Although the light was fading her hair still shone – and there was a lustre to her skin and eyes. Raffles' loss was my gain again in terms of spending the afternoon with this modern day Portia – although I knew I would lose her to him in an instant should he so desire it. I was a lead casket to his gold.

"Bunny, you are wonderfully sweet. Whatever happens between Raffles and I, I would like us to remain friends."

"I would like that too," I declared. Although I did not declare how I would have equally liked a large gin and tonic at that moment.

Chapter Nine

I felt both ten feet tall – and also like I was about to collapse from my legs giving way – as Lucy took my arm when we walked back to the house. She went directly upstairs, saying she had to change, as we entered. No sooner had she vanished when a shiny-faced servant appeared and asked me if I could join Lord Rosebery – along with Mister Raffles – in the drawing room. He led the way, in shoes even shinier than his face. Gorgeous portraits by Stubbs and Gainsborough hung upon the walls. When I asked our host over the weekend what he thought of Impressionism he curtly described it as being 'a hideous collection of wretched daubs'. I was too polite, or rather frightened, to argue. The house was also populated by all sorts of sporting memorabilia and antiques which glowed with exquisiteness and homeliness.

I heard the roar of laughter – and the roar of a fire – before I even entered the room. Lord Rosebery immediately got up to address me.

"Mister Manders, welcome." His voice was rich and deep. His head was large and his face was round with what I can only describe as puppy fat. If I was being polite I would have called him well built. If I was being accurate however I would have said our former Prime Minister was corpulent. Two inscrutable light blue eyes were rimmed with the redness of sleeplessness. He wore a morning suit of dark serge that, although doubtless expensive, did not seem so.

"Thank you for inviting me, Lord Rosebery."

"I shall cut a deal with you Mister Manders. I trust you will be more amenable to negotiation and compromise than the Tories and Liberal Party. But if I am allowed to call you Bunny, then you can call me Archie, or just plain Rosebery."

There was a charm to his manner, but yet the request was still tantamount to a patrician order.

"Archie it is," I replied as we shook hands. As we did so, Rosebery gave a subtle nod of his head and I was soon in possession of a gin and tonic.

"I hope that your walk around the grounds was as pleasant as the company you kept," Rosebery remarked as we sat down. Raffles was ensconced in a chair by the fire, cradling a whisky and soda-water – perfectly at ease with the surroundings and auspicious company.

"Yes. Thankfully the weather is still mild for this time of year," I answered, boring myself as well as my host.

"Lucy is a lovely girl. Although I fear her radicalism may turn me into more of a conservative, sooner or later. But she is both sensible and progressive for the most part – albeit one cannot and should not always marry those two words together. She is very fond of you, Raffles. I'm not sure how many times I have

RICHARD FOREMAN

had to slyly change the subject when she has started to yammer on about you," Rosebery drily exclaimed, whilst slyly smiling at Raffles.

"I would have done the very same. Even I often change the subject when someone talks about me, to me. Else I might fall asleep," Raffles drily responded, with his own species of a sly smile upon his face. He could not have known our host for more than an hour, but anyone might have believed that the two men had known each other for years – such was their familiarity and shared sense of humour. "I hope you had a nice afternoon too though Bunny, though doubtless you are glad to see the vista before you of a gin and tonic in your hand. How was Lucy?"

"You can ask her herself," a voice chimed in from behind me.

My mouth was slightly agape from being just about to speak, but also the figure behind the voice looked jaw-droppingly beautiful. I had little time to marvel at how swiftly she had changed, for I was too busy marvelling at the black silk evening dress that she had changed into. She wore little make-up, for nature endowed her with enough beauty. Her hair was pinned up, but a few curls hung down like the myrtle in the garden. I was momentarily speechless.

"Women's enfranchisement would progress a lot quicker if more of the suffragettes possessed your wardrobe, as well as views," Raffles remarked, smiling behind a haze of cigarette smoke.

Lucy's instant reaction was to both blush and smile, for I suspect she had changed to make a desired impression on Raffles, and she glowed with satisfaction. But then she chided Raffles by saying that the suffragette movement was a campaign of substance, not style. My friend merely shrugged and turned his gaze towards the fireplace again. I however could not take my eyes of Lucy. Not that she noticed however, as she could not take her eyes off Raffles – as though he were a poem that she could not quite work out the meaning of.

Chapter Ten

After another drink or two we had a fine dinner, accompanied by even finer wines. Finer still was the company, as I found myself sitting next to Lucy. I sensed she may have been disappointed not to be seated next to Raffles — but yet I was pleased enough for the both of us to be sat next to her. Raffles spent most of the evening deep in conversation with Rosebery. As captivated as I was by my dinner companion I could not help but be distracted on occasion by their discussions. First they spoke about literature, with both agreeing that the great novels of the century by French and Russian authors eclipsed those written by British novelists. Of Flaubert and *A Sentimental Education* our host remarked, whilst fixing his gaze at Raffles intently, "There is one fine moral pervading every page: the emptiness of a life of pleasure." My friend nodded his head, albeit I am not sure how much he would have agreed with our host. What they disagreed in earnest about was the greatness of Napoleon.

"Wellington did not win the battle of Waterloo. Rather, Napoleon lost it," Rosebery staunchly argued.

"If you are to argue that ultimately Napoleon defeated

Napoleon, I'm content with that. The main thing is that he was defeated. He was a great tyrant, rather than great man, who turned Europe into a charnel house," Raffles countered.

But Napoleon was one of only a few things that the pair disagreed upon. I do not believe that Raffles needed to even play a part when he sympathised with Rosebery's politics, taste in literature, and wry sense of humour. Such was the mutual good feeling between the two of them that I even dared to hope that Raffles might desist in his plan to rob our generous host. Yet, when Lucy and Rosebery were briefly both away from the table, my hopes were dashed as quickly as a socialist can delude himself.

"Tonight's the night old chap. I'm worried that we may have a house full of restless revellers tomorrow evening. Stay awake. Opportunity – and I – will come knocking upon your door in a few hours."

Shortly afterwards Raffles excused himself, explaining that he was tired. Rosebery excused himself also, fearing that he might be left alone in the awkward and unwelcome position of staying up with this dullard. Yet Lucy and I remained chatting for some time afterwards, till she finally took pity on the staff. She spoke of another visit to London and I promised to take her to a new, critically acclaimed production of Richard II.

"The soliloquy at the end is my favourite, from all of Shakespeare," she enthused.

"Love to Richard is a strange brooch in this all-hating world," I quoted, with perhaps a little too much conviction in my performance. The drink had loosened my lips, or soul. Lucy tilted her head slightly, offered me a sympathetic smile and reached out to take me by the hand. Before she could say anything however a servant entered and asked us if we wanted anything else. I could not quite decide whether I welcomed his appearance or not.

"I could invite Raffles also to the play," I mentioned.

"No, I wish to go with my new friend. But I hope that my new friend will now forgive me for abandoning him. I should go to bed. Thank you for a lovely evening, Bunny," she warmly expressed and bent down and kissed me on the cheek – in a sisterly way more than anything, I judged.

Whether it was the lingering tingling sensation upon my cheek or the butterflies in my stomach from the imminent job with Raffles which kept sleep at bay, I was duly wide awake when I heard the knock upon my door.

Chapter Eleven

For a brief, tantalising moment I imagined that it might have been Lucy knocking upon my bedroom door - but it was Raffles. His eyes shone, akin to the look he had when he would go out to bat – sensing that there was a big score to be had. We were both in our dressing gowns, although my companion's garment had special inside pockets sown into it to conceal loot.

I pleaded with Raffles again to desist in his plan, arguing that we were biting the hand that fed us this evening, that Rosebery had shown us nothing but kindness, that if apprehended we might despoil Lucy's name too.

"Rosebery enriched me with his company this evening Bunny, I grant you. But his valuables will enrich me even more," he replied with devilment in his expression.

"You can be your own worst enemy sometimes," I replied in earnest. I also thought him callous in not even addressing the predicament that our larceny could put Lucy in.

"I know. But thankfully I have you as a friend old chap to compensate for my faults," he countered, smiling and attempting to puncture my seriousness.

Raffles had an answer, or witticism which could serve as an answer, for everything. It seems that our hushed discussion was over however as he proceeded to walk off, in pursuit of boodle. My eyes were growing accustomed to the dark, as my conscience had grown accustomed to turning a blind eye to my friend's sins (and consequently my own).

I duly pursued Raffles. In part, because I hoped to still dissuade him from his course of action. In part, out of loyalty and friendship. And in part selfishly, for somewhere in the crevices of my soul my adventures with Raffles made me feel alive. Was he some kind of Pied Piper or Siren? Or was I a more willing Sancho Panza to his Don Quixote? Let us not forget also that our life of crime did not just finance Raffles' enviable lifestyle. Yet for how long could we continue to ride our luck? I continually posed this question to myself – especially during a job. I even occasionally wished for our capture, for then I would be free from the constant anxiety of dwelling upon getting caught. Yet I also fancied that, if incarcerated with Raffles, then things would not be all bad – though I feared that the food would not prove as morish as the company.

Yet one should be careful for what one wishes for. No sooner did this train of thought idly trammel through my mind than a light came on – and I nearly blacked out from shock and terror. Was the game finally up, rather than afoot?

Chapter Twelve

"Are you having trouble sleeping too, gentlemen?"

Rosebery seemed to briefly scrutinise why his two guests should be creeping around in the dark at such an hour but having the pleasure of our company appeared to trump any feelings of curiosity or suspicion.

"Come, I wish to show you my home within my home, my sanctuary. It's where I keep all my most prized treasures," our host exclaimed, his deep voice sounding somewhat child-like for once. Rosebery led us down a corridor and grinned as he opened a door and switched on the light – to his library.

Our eyes were stapled open and we were awestruck, more so than if canvases by Stubbs and Gainsborough – or Turner or Titian – were lining the walls. Books and manuscripts sprouted out upon shelves and tables, volumes of all differing sizes and hues. Goosebumps appeared of my skin, more from excitement than the chilled air. Not even King Solomon's mines contained such riches. The room was the largest in the house, I warrant. Yet it was largely used by just one man. Gladstone had called Rosebery's library one of the finest in the country. Although a number of my articles may testify to how much I disagreed with the old man on political grounds, I could not contradict him on this matter. A fire hummed in the background and a few clinks could be heard as Rosebery poured us each a glass of claret. Yet a reverent silence pervaded the air as Raffles and I reached for various books rather than our wine glasses, as we each took a tour of the chamber like children in a toy shop. Or we were worshipers in a temple, having found our Holy of Holies.

I discovered a signed first edition of Hume's History of England, a volume of Goethe with a personal inscription by Napoleon, signed books and letters by Hugo, Wellington, Pitt, Swift and Newton. The jewels in the crown were a First Folio and King Charles I's copy of *The Book of Common Prayer*. I gazed over to my companion and watched him lovingly stroke spines and covers, more so than if he were holding a necklace or priceless cameo in his hands.

We finally sat down with our host by the fire.

"Cicero said that a home without books is like a body without a soul. If so, then you have quite the soulful home, Archie," Raffles remarked, shaking his head again in wonderment and lighting a Sullivan.

"Hmm, Cicero. You have a good name for a horse there Raffles."

Thankfully the conversation turned towards literature, rather than the turf, given our surroundings. Rosebery came out with a statement which I shall never forget, although I am not the best judge I dare say as to how much I have heeded his advice over the years.

"The curse of great novelists as a rule is that after their first success or successes they become inebriated with their triumph and attempt a higher flight in which they are lost in the clouds and become diffuse, or philosophical or what. In this foolish ambition, they drop their own gift, that of telling a story."

The conversation finally veered away from literature when Raffles asked about a small, attractive sapphire locket which Rosebery often clasped – and then placed upon the table – and then re-clasped. Our host paused and looked pensive, or pained even, before answering.

"On the third of January, 1878, at 4.20 I used this locket to propose to Hannah, my late wife. Love – and I must confess not a little alcohol – fuelled my leap of faith. Benjamin Franklin once advised that one should keep one's eyes wide open before marriage, and half shut afterwards. But I cannot share the cynicism of the great man. I cared for my wife and admired her every day, in an ever-increasing fashion. I have a farrier who often describes his wife as his 'other half'. Hannah however was my better half."

I am ashamed to say that I dozed off shortly after this. Tiredness and the wine got the better of me. When I woke – and I cannot accurately say how long I was asleep for – the widower was still talking about his wife and was growing even more emotional. Ever one to avoid emotional or awkward scenes I pretended to still be asleep – and heard Rosebery recount one of the last conversations he had with his late wife, who had died from typhoid over half a decade ago.

"'Do you think I shall ever pull through?' – Hannah asked. I could not lie to her, so I replied that I hoped so. She then remarked, "How short everything is in life, when I think of how you came to Mentmore and brought me the sapphire locket. No one could have made me as happy as you. I sometimes have felt it was wrong that I thought of the children so little in comparison to you. I will try to live for you. Some years hence you may care for someone else – you may forget me. It seems so strange that I should think so much of this: what she may be like. How dreadful it would be if it were the other way." I replied in earnest by saying that I had prayed to God that he would take me instead of her. She responded, affectionately and sincerely, "That would never do. I could never live a day after you."

As much as I was glad of my decision to pretend to remain asleep, such was the broken emotion in Rosebery's tone – and my desire to witness Raffles' reaction to this confession – that I subtly lifted one eye to take in the scene as our host gently remarked,

"When she died our happy home was a wreck, her children were motherless and I had lost the best wife man ever had. I did not – nor do not – see the elements of consolation, except in the memory of her beautiful, unselfish life."

Tears ran down Rosebery's otherwise still face, as he mournfully gazed into the fire. If this portrait did not sadden me enough, I then looked over at my dearest of friends to find tears glistening upon his cheeks, too. It was the first time that I had ever witnessed Raffles cry. I thought him incapable of tears, in a similar way that

I thought him incapable of ever wearing an ill-cut suit. Yet he grimly stared into the fire too, either in sympathy with our host's grief – or in mourning for someone dear to him.

Chapter Thirteen

Eventually I woke up 'for real', once my companions had sufficiently altered the topic of conversation. We all then retired to our rooms shortly after that. What with the servants commencing their chores, Raffles' window in having the house to himself closed. I slept fitfully, with all manner of thoughts disturbing my rest.

As the dawn began to pour marmalade coloured light through my window I got up to survey the scene outside. A sea of silvery mist covered the parkland, dulling the greenery but furnishing the landscape with a picturesque beauty all the same. Below me on the veranda, wreathed in the morning mist, stood an enigmatic Rosebery. He was gazing out into the distance. One could not tell whether he was dwelling upon the past, present or future – if hope or despondency was colouring his thoughts. His mood was not just disguised by the mist. It struck me there and then that, in his unpredictability and inscrutable character, he was akin to Raffles. Raffles remarked, shortly after that weekend, that nobody could divine what Rosebery desired, because he did not know himself. Or he desired so many things as make any one thing suffer from a loss of focus. Or he ultimately desired the impossible – the love of his life back. The thought duly crossed my mind that my friend could have been referring to himself, rather than our host, in some respects.

I went back to bed and understandably rose quite late. Whilst Raffles and Rosebery took part in a weekly football match near the stables with the staff I happily hid myself away in the library – although my happiness duly increased in being discovered, by Lucy. We chatted for a while, but then a comfortable silence passed between us as we each buried our heads in a book. I could not sometimes help however peer out from behind my copy of Milton to gaze at my companion – and bask in her prettiness.

A constant stream of guests commenced to arrive from mid-afternoon onwards. Curiosity eventually got the better of Lucy and she disappeared to discover who would be joining us for dinner that evening. Half an hour or so later she returned, breathless yet glowing. She rattled off a list of guests, including the Asquiths, Earl Spencer, a couple of Barings, the editors of The Daily Mail and the Fortnightly Review, a close relation of Otto von Bismarck, a distant relation of our Queen and, heaven help us, the Archbishop of Canterbury. She also added that Sidney and Beatrice Webb, the founders of the new fangled Fabian movement, had just arrived. I did not share Lucy's delight in the prospect of meeting them. I prayed, to a God that the two men were forever haranguing people not to believe in, that H.G. Wells and George Bernard Shaw – two acolytes of the Fabian religion – were not joining us also for dinner. Thankfully my prayers were answered. Raffles shared my distrust and disdain for the Webbs. Whilst having a glass of wine, before we went in to the dining room, he remarked,

"I sincerely hope that I'm not seated anywhere near them at dinner, Bunny. They may well hold themselves up as fine examples of the Anglo-Saxon race but I hold them – and their racist views – in contempt." At dinner I overheard Sidney Webb exclaim that 'the country is gradually falling to the Irish and Jews.' I was tempted to reply that there would be then little left for the trade unions and socialists to ruin, but I desisted.

The dishes were as varied as the quality of company at dinner. The highlights of the meal were the gravlax salmon, roasted grouse and cuts of Highland beef. Fortunately Raffles and I were seated away from the Webbs and other political undesirables. Yet we were sat some spaces apart from each other still. He was close to the head of the table, near our host, whilst I sat next to Lucy a few places down. Out of the corner of my eye I could not help but notice how Raffles, as well as Rosebery, held court. He batted back some witty answers in regards to questions about cricket and a small audience marvelled at how quickly he could spin an apple off his finger and catch it (even with his eyes closed) each time it fell. He also found time to be considerate – or one might judge flirtatious – with a serving maid who a gruff guest had been rude to. I thought that Lucy might think him honourable for such behaviour – as Emma did Mr Knightley for dancing with Harriet Smith when she had been slighted. Or I conversely wondered if she might suffer pangs of jealousy as a result of Raffles' conduct.

But she genuinely – and happily – took little notice of my friend at dinner. Chiefly Lucy spent her time keeping me entertained – and enchanted – during our meal. And I like to think I entertained, and maybe even enchanted her, in return.

"We are sharing the same table Bunny as some of the most powerful politicians in the land," she uttered in genuine awe, albeit I hope I also traced a satirical note to her tone. We were only in the company of the Liberal Party after all.

"As long as they don't share their opinions with us as well," I drily replied.

"Have you never thought about being a politician yourself – and campaigning for a seat?"

"No, the only seat I desire at the moment Lucy is this one, next to you."

And she here smiled that smile that made me smile. I feared that I was falling and spinning too, although it was unlikely that anyone, let alone Raffles, could catch me.

As much as it might have been a pleasure to do so, I could not devote myself entirely to Lucy and ignore the other dinner guests around me. Shortly after the above exchange I found myself chatting to a lean, dark-eyed fellow opposite me who I vaguely recognised, but couldn't quite place. I fancied I had seen his picture in a newspaper. He had ferret like features and an energetic manner – albeit this was also coupled with nervousness, as though he were overly conscious of the society he was keeping. He was doubtless dressed in his best attire, although it was still the most poorly fashioned around the table.

"Someone tells me that you're a friend of that Mr Raffles, the cricketer over there. I once saw him play at Lords. Not even the good Doctor had a remedy to combat his spin bowling that day. And your name is?"

"Harry Manders, but people call me Bunny. And yours?"

"Inspector Lestrade, of Scotland Yard."

Chapter Fourteen

For a moment it felt like the grouse I had eaten had come to life again and wanted to fly from my stomach, up through my throat and exit back out of my mouth. I gulped, as though wishing to swallow the bird back down.

"Oh, are you the Inspector Lestrade?" I asked, innocently.

"Yes, the one who has assisted Mr Sherlock Holmes with some of his cases. Or rather I could argue that he has assisted me."

I thought it prudent not to mention that I had had my own dealings with Mr Holmes, which can be found in the episode of *Raffles: The Gentleman Thief.*

"What brings you to The Durdans then, Inspector? You are not here on business I hope."

I tried to act casually, but I refrained from lighting a Sullivan in fear that my hand would tremble whilst smoking it.

"Well Lord Rosebery kindly invited me. I used to be a point of contact for him when he headed the London County Council. But between you and me Mr Manders, Holmes tipped me the wink that a notorious burglar might be paying the house a visit this weekend. He said that a little bird had told him. Doubtless it was one of his Baker Street Irregulars."

"Oh, is that so? Your secret will be safe with me, Inspector."

Despite my worry that my legs might give way if I stood up I smiled politely and excused myself.

Raffles and I had a signal, that of bending down to tie one's shoelace, whenever one of us wanted to urgently speak with the other. I duly pretended to tie my shoe within Raffles' view and he promptly joined me in the hallway.

"Really?" Raffles calmly replied upon hearing my news, appearing mildly intrigued rather than concerned. I dare say I looked concerned for the both of us however. A film of sweat glazed over my entire countenance and I probably needed the help of Raffles' jemmy to un-knit my brow.

"We must not do anything rash. We must act naturally."

"I intend to Bunny. I will indeed do what comes naturally to me," Raffles replied, his teeth gleaming in a smile behind a plume of cigarette smoke.

"No, I must put my foot down!" I exclaimed in an excitable whisper. To my shame I even stamped my foot down like a child in a tantrum. "We cannot risk capture." I was going to add that I could not risk losing Lucy, but I justly realised that she was not mine to lose. If anything, she was Raffles'.

But I might as well have asked him to give up smoking, or drinking his customary whisky and soda before bed. He was as constant as the northern star in his addiction to larceny.

"Look upon Lestrade as a challenge to be overcome, rather than as an insurmountable obstacle, Bunny. Where's the sport in scoring a goal into an open net? And if I cannot outwit Inspector Lestrade, then I deserve to be apprehended."

"But Holmes —"

"Is at home, thinking about his supper rather than dwelling upon us. We are small enough fish to slip through his net. Remember, he had a bigger fish to fry — that Moriarty chap. There must be some misunderstanding on Lestrade's part. It would not be the first time, from what I've read.

"A.J, please," I unashamedly begged, again akin to a small child.

Such was my piteous expression that for a moment I believed that Raffles might indeed relent. But Raffles was Raffles.

"I'm sorry old chap, but as you yourself have stated — when all else is written, I am a villain."

Chapter Fifteen

Dessert was served. There was not a sweet pastry or crème brulee in the whole of Surrey, or heaven even, which could have removed the bitter taste from my mouth however. I had merely walked off in sullen silence after my exchange with Raffles. We all retreated into the house's largest drawing room for drinks after dinner. I attempted to stay in the vicinity of Raffles whilst also keeping an eye on Inspector Lestrade, whilst trying to still devote myself to Lucy. I have never been so exhausted whilst just standing still at a party before, working my way through half a bottle of vintage port. Rosebery held court again, rightly deflecting any questions about politics. When asked what his political motto was our host replied, "My political motto is, I don't give a damn." But Rosebery happily discussed any and everything else – including football.

"You were a wolf in sheep's clothing today, Raffles. You said that you did not care for football, but you were arguably the best player on the field. You set up two goals and scored another."

"I can assure you that I still care little for football. To run about constantly for forty-five minutes – twice - chasing a ball, without being able to stop and have a cigarette, seems barbarous. C.B. Fry however often roped me into playing whilst he trained at Southampton. I picked up the odd trick, although the sum of my skills pale in comparison to the number of bruises I collected on my shins."

Rosebery broke out into a deep, rich laugh.

"I keep meaning to invite Fry to one of my parties," he finally replied.

"You should. I recommend you pick him for your team should you arrange another football match, too. Also, you may wish to invite him up without his wife. She is his other, rather than better, half," Raffles wryly remarked. The reference to Rosebery's comment the night before seemed to provoke a remembrance of other confessions and the two men shared a brief, private moment.

"You are a superior inside, Raffles, despite your indifference to the game. You are also a good friend," Rosebery remarked whilst warmly clasping him by the arm. Raffles similarly gazed at his host with genuine affection and admiration. Despite his son having played for Surrey, Rosebery it turned out was indifferent to the game of cricket. Raffles duly offered to try and fix this error by giving a display of batting and bowling for the following day.

By this time another guest had whisked Lucy away from me. Perhaps she had rightly grown tired of my distracted mood. My rival was as handsome as he was titled. His manner was as oily as his hair and the only thing he loved more than his appearance was the sound of his own voice. Suffice to say the Tory Party were expecting great things from him. Partly stressed, partly disconsolate, partly drunk, I decided to take some air.

To cap off my miseries I discovered that I was out of cigarettes. Instead of a row of Sullivans my own melancholy face stared up at me from the silver cigarette case. Loneliness gripped around my pea-sized heart like a vice. Raffles had put his villainy before our friendship. I was dreaming to think that I could have a serious chance to court – and win – Lucy. I had merely mistaken politeness for attraction. I was perhaps as low as when I had turned up at Raffles' apartment all those months ago and threatened to end it all.

"You look like you could use some company, or at least a Sullivan," her sweet voice intoned. Lucy passed me a cigarette. "It's a beautiful night."

As ever, she was right. A velvety black sky, sequined with stars, shone glossily above us. I immediately took my coat off and placed it around her shivering – and shimmering – shoulders. We sat upon a bench on the veranda.

"If you need to get back to the party, I'll be fine. This is a golden opportunity for you to lobby the men who matter in regards to women's suffrage."

"No. I'm afraid that you are going to have to suffer my company some more, Mr Harry Manders. Women may need the vote, but what I want right now is to spend time with you."

Lucy looked up at me and smiled, the light in her eyes eclipsing that of the stars above. She laced her fingers into mine – and we kissed.

Chapter Sixteen

I could not rightly say how much time elapsed before Lucy and I returned to the party but most of the guests had still yet to retire to bed. Raffles smiled and pulled a face upon seeing Lucy's arm curled around mine. I blushed, but was glowing more so from happiness. Lucy went to bed not long after we re-entered the drawing room however.

"Thank you for a lovely evening Miss Rosebery," I remarked whilst we were in the company of others. But we were in a world of our own still.

"And thank you, Mr Manders, just for being you. I very much enjoyed our conversation on the veranda. I look forward to having a similar chat tomorrow."

After watching Lucy gracefully work her way through a throng of guests and leave I turned around to witness Raffles talking to Lestrade. I sometimes thought my friend as mischievous as Puck, or as arrogant as a Caesar. As fretful as a Polonius I hurriedly walked over to the pair.

"Yes, I spoke to Miss Rosebery at dinner. She was sitting near me. She was charming, although I understand that she is one of those suffragettes," Lestrade exclaimed, wrinkling his nose up in either disdain or incomprehension. "I was at a briefing the other day at the Yard. Some fellow warned that these women might one day become militant in order to have their demands met and set off bombs and chain themselves to buildings or railings. My fear is not that one of these mad women would chain themselves to railings, but rather my worry is that once shackled there someone would then try and free her," the Inspector then posited, either in jest or in earnest.

"If only the fellow you are after would conveniently chain himself to a railing to await his arrest, Inspector. What can you tell us about him?" Raffles asked, seemingly more concerned with scratching a tiny gravy stain off of his lapel than being interested in Lestrade's task.

"Not much, I'm afraid, gentlemen. I have been informed that he may be wearing a disguise – and that he usually works with an accomplice. And he is as intelligent as he is daring, Holmes remarked. But myself, Constable Dickinson and the rest of my men will not just be his equal, but superior."

"Perhaps Mr Holmes could be mistaken in his judgement."

"I have never known Mr Holmes to be wrong. As sure as day follows night his judgement has been sound over the years, although his methods have sometimes proved unorthodox."

"Well, Inspector Lestrade, day will soon follow night again. But I should get some sleep before morning. Please do call upon me though should you and Constable Dickinson need any assistance in apprehending your felon. As Mr Holmes will doubtless tell you, it takes a thief to catch a thief. And I have stolen the odd heart and taken the odd wicket over the years," Raffles remarked with a wink.

Chapter Seventeen

"You are under arrest!"

I had been dreading, yet in some ways also expecting, hearing those words for some months now. Finally they rang in my ears. My heart sank, but yet also went out to my friend. Should Raffles have attempted to escape I dare say I would have tackled any pursuer to the ground. If Inspector Lestrade could have looked any more self-satisfied, then I warrant he may well have exploded. And damn Sherlock Holmes, I thought to myself in the heat of the moment. I glanced over at Raffles. He looked confused rather than guilty. I dare say I looked both confused and guilty. Were Constable Dickinson's words meant for me too, I wondered, or just for Raffles? Was this the end for us both?

But I am getting a little ahead of myself. In regards to the night before Lestrade and I retired not long after Raffles, with the Inspector checking in one last time with his men.

I woke to have a late breakfast. A number of guests from the party had already departed. Raffles was nowhere to be seen. After breakfast I retreated into the library again, where Lucy was waiting for me. We happily spent a few hours just idly conversing and reading, like an old married couple almost. We read over a number of letters by John Stuart Mill and Harriet Taylor. She asked me that if I could be gifted just one book or letter from the library, which would I take? My first thought was, of course, for Shakespeare's First Folio. I was also going to reply that I would choose a simple note, one which Lucy would write – containing her address. But in the end I decided upon the most valuable book being a first edition of Smith's The Wealth of Nations. When I asked the same question of Lucy in return, she immediately picked the first edition copy of Mary Wollstonecraft's *A Vindication of the Rights of Woman.*" I felt vindicated in not commenting about the choice. I briefly here thought too about which book Raffles would select, and recalled the way he held up the inscribed volume of Byron's poetry with awe and visible pleasure on Friday evening.

It was now mid afternoon. Nearly all the guests had departed, but Raffles duly kept his promise to give a display of spin bowling on the lawn outside the front of the house. By the end only Rosebery, Raffles, Lucy, Lestrade and myself remained. It was when we were all walking back that I heard Constable Dickinson's scorching voice. As mentioned I first looked to Lestrade and Raffles, before noticing that they were both glaring at Constable Dickinson – who was hauling Jack Shanks across the grounds, flanked by two other constables.

Shanks had dyed his hair and was dressed as a stable boy but I still recognised him by his compact build, green eyes and roguish features. My joy at our apparent reprieve was short-lived, as I feared that Shanks might recognise us from our encounter in

Limehouse. As Lestrade revelled in his triumph Shanks merely just gazed at Raffles, in a similar askance way to when he had stood before him in the public house – sizing him up and trying to place him. But it seemed that the house-breaker could put two and two together about as well as our Chancellor of the Exchequer – and things didn't quite add up for him.

"I found him with these," Dickinson announced, retrieving a handful of jewellery from his pocket. "And he tried to take this," he added, extracting Rosebery's sapphire locket from his trousers. Our host gasped – and if he did not look upon Shanks with contempt before, he did now. Yet Rosebery's look of disdain was quickly usurped by one of fear, as Shanks swiftly pulled out a revolver which had been strapped to his ankle. Either I instinctively moved in front of Lucy, or she retreated behind me.

"And I'll be taking it back, if you don't mind," Shanks impudently remarked, pointing the gun between Lestrade and our host. Shanks also took Lestrade's revolver. He then instructed me to tie the shoelaces of the policemen's footwear together – and so as to both embarrass them and impede any pursuit I pulled their trousers down around their ankles. I noticed Raffles raised a corner of his mouth in a smirk at this.

"Now I hope you gents won't try and be heroes. It'll be difficult to get blood and gunpowder out of those togs," Shanks warned, addressing Raffles, Rosebery and myself.

"I'll not intervene, on condition that you give this gentleman his sapphire locket back. It possesses more than just a monetary value to my friend," Raffles politely and calmly expressed, albeit there was steel as well as silk in his tone.

"You'll not intervene, fella, due to the condition that I'll put a bullet through your guts if you do," Shanks replied, baring his teeth in a sneer. Raffles merely shook his head in reply, as if disappointed with someone who was being discourteous, rather than villainous.

"Give my regards to Sherlock Holmes, Lestrade. Tell him this is one hound that he won't track down," the cracksman triumphantly exclaimed, walking backwards whilst still pointing his gun at us. When believing it safe to do so however Jack Shanks turned and sprinted across the grounds towards the gates to the property. Her Majesty's finest commenced to pull up their trousers, with one of the constables toppling over as he did so. But I paid the policeman little heed, transfixed as I was by one of the most remarkable feats I have ever witnessed in my life.

Raffles seemed to pause for but a few seconds to take into account the speed and direction of his target. He briefly gazed up at the sky, either in a fleeting prayer or to assess the wind, before launching the cricket ball he was holding into the air. The red dot arched across the pale blue background. I stood amazed, my mouth agape, in light of just my friend's audacious attempt. Yet try to imagine – you'll have to, as this writer is lost for words – how I felt when I observed the ball strike the felon upon the back of his head and render him unconscious.

"I think he's out," Raffles remarked.

Chapter Eighteen

We just all stood there stunned at first, albeit not quite as stunned in the same way that Shanks had been. Hands were soon clapping Raffles upon the back though and praise and comments of wonderment were gunned out and colouring the air. Rosebery was also particularly touched and grateful upon getting his sapphire locket back. Yet Raffles himself acted with modesty, or indifference even, towards his astonishing feat. Perhaps he did not wish to revel in the glory of his actions also due to the fact that he had helped to apprehend a fellow thief.

"This will make a fine story for the newspapers, if they'll believe it," Lestrade proclaimed, smiling as he envisioned his name in print again.

"I would rather that my name be kept out of the newspapers for this particular piece of fielding, if you do not mind, Inspector. Now, rather than catch a thief, we must be conscious now Bunny of catching our train."

Rosebery entreated us to stay another night, which I was not averse to, but Raffles explained that he had arranged to have lunch at noon with a friend, Ranji, the next day. Whilst Raffles and our host shared one last drink and cigar, Lucy and I said our goodbyes in the garden. Much remained unsaid in many ways, but we promised to write to one another and I promised to travel down to Truro at the earliest opportunity. Again, we kissed.

As much as I wanted to discuss all manner of things with my friend on the journey home I fell asleep both on the train and in the hansom cab in London. I accompanied Raffles back to the Albany however. I lit a fire whilst he lit another candle upon his desk. He then briefly disappeared, to return with a bottle of Pol Roger and two glasses.

"In victory, deserve it. In defeat, need it," he announced as he poured the champagne.

"I am sorry that you were defeated this weekend A.J, that you did not make a score on your perfect wicket. Please forgive me if I was in some way responsible."

"I am drinking in light of a victory, as well as a defeat old chap."

"How so?" I replied, my face creased in bemusement.

"Dear Bunny, I must confess that I did indeed venture down to The Durdans this weekend in order to make a score so to speak, upon a perfect wicket. Yet circumstances conspired against me."

"So where is your victory?"

"You do not have a conniving bone in your body, do you my friend? Thankfully, for you, I have several. My lack of being unable to steal any loot this weekend has been more than compensated by the fact that you have stolen Lucy Rosebery's heart. I've suspected that you've had feelings for her for some time. This weekend was your perfect wicket old chap – and I like to think that I acted as the grounds man. Firstly, do you think that those new clothes I bought you earlier in the week were for the intention of impressing Rosebery? Also, I dare say you thought me a little rude, or callous, in my avoidance of Lucy this weekend. Yet every hour spent apart from me meant that she could spend that time with you. And who do you think snuck into the dining room and moved the place cards so that you could sit next to your intended last night?" Raffles exclaimed with a twinkle in his eye, whilst lighting another Sullivan.

I could have been angry and frustrated again with my friend for keeping me in the dark as to his plans, but I wasn't. For Cupid's aim had been as accurate as Raffles' throwing arm.

"You are a devil A.J, as well as an angel. Thank you. I hope indeed I have stolen Lucy's heart. She has certainly stolen mine."

"I did not altogether return empty handed from The Durdans either, old chap. But you'll be pleased to know that I was given the valuable item, as opposed to having stolen it, as a thank you for my actions."

Raffles here walked over to his luggage and retrieved the inscribed volume of Byron's book of verse that he had revered so much in the library. I handled the book with similar reverence and read the inscription that Rosebery had added, with a line of thanks to accompany the quote by Virgil.

'Facilis descensus Averno:
Noctes atque dies patet atri ianua Ditis;
Sed revocare gradum superasque evader ad auras,

Hop opus, his labor est.'

"This is one spoil that you won't be taking to Spokes to sell on. May I inscribe something myself though A. J?"

"Certainly old chap."

I wrote the following and then handed the book back to Raffles.

"*When all else is written, you are not altogether a villain. Bunny.*"

He smiled.

RAFFLES:

CAUGHT OUT

Chapter One

The following episode occurred shortly after the events recounted in *Raffles: A Perfect Wicket*. I had just returned from a day trip down to Truro, where I had visited my intended (albeit I had yet to formally propose; it had not even been a week since Lucy Rosebery and I had started courting). I came back to my apartment from the train station to find a note from Raffles, requesting that I call upon him at the Albany, regardless of the lateness of the hour. Although fatigued from a long (but wonderfully enjoyable) day I duly assented to my friend's request and headed over to Piccadilly without even stopping to change clothes. I was partly curious as to what could inspire a sense of urgency in my usually laidback friend – and I was still brimming with gratitude towards Raffles for having helped play Cupid in regards to Lucy and I.

Although it was approaching midnight Raffles was still awake. He opened the door and soon set me up with a Sullivan and a large gin and tonic.

"I'm pleased to see that you are getting some wear out of the outfit I bought you for our recent trip to The Durdans. I do not remember the collar being smeared with so much lipstick when first purchasing the shirt however," Raffles remarked, raising his eyebrow suggestively.

I immediately blushed, my face turning as red as any shade of lipstick, and was about to rush to the toilet to inspect and remove the mark when Raffles let out a laugh.

"Forgive me Bunny, I am but jesting. Your collar remains as spotless as your honour old chap. Tell me, how was your trip? Is Lucy well?"

"Lucy is well and sends her regards. I had a lovely time, with the loveliest of women," I replied, the warm glow in my expression coming as much from recalling Lucy as it did from the first gin and tonic of the night. I decided not to dwell upon how my time spent with Lucy's father had proved less than lovely however. I felt like I was in the company of my accountant rather than a prospective father-in-law at times, as he interrogated me about my income and prospects. I warrant my stock went down when he heard what little stock I possessed – and he also looked decidedly unimpressed when I revealed how I owned square footage, as opposed to acreage.

"I'm pleased for you, old chap. But I have not just invited you over to convey how happy I am for you, Bunny."

"Do you wish to discuss a job?" I asked, surprising myself by my eagerness.

"It is more a favour, for a mutual friend. As you know, I recently had lunch with Ranji."

Ranji was K. S. Ransjitsinhji, arguably the finest batsman of the age. I had last seen Ranji a week before, having bumped into him outside the Cafe Royal. It was there, appearing somewhat distraught, that he had asked if he could meet up with Raffles at the earliest convenience.

"How was he?"

"He has been better, Bunny. It seems that Ranji has compromised himself with a woman. I am going to give our friend the benefit of the doubt when he says that he was unaware of the true station of the lady in question, one Iris Adams, when he became involved with her. It is not like Ranji to lose his heart, or his wicket, easily. It seems he lost his head too somewhat during their brief affair and he gave this Iris Adams a valuable ruby encrusted ring as a token of his esteem. This ring however was not his to give. It technically belongs still to Ranji's home province in India of Nawanagar – and should have only been gifted to a future bride. The affair has ended now however. Ranji has written to Mrs Adams – she calls herself such, being a widow – and has asked her to return the ring but to no avail. He has even offered her a sum of money, but the lady still declines to give the ring back. Hence Ranji has asked me to intercede on his behalf and visit Mrs Adams. I have an appointment with her tomorrow, at 11.00. I am hoping that you will be free to join me, Bunny."

"Of course. I'm happy to help in any way I can. Do you believe that you will be able to convince Mrs Adams to return the ring?"

"Let's just say that the favour could ultimately turn into a job," Raffles replied, after taking another sip of his whisky and soda-water, his eyes twinkling as much as any ruby encrusted ring.

Chapter Two

I was not sure whether it was due to the cab juddering upon the cobblestones, or my shivering from the nip in the air, but my teeth couldn't help but chatter as I listened to Raffles divulge some more information about the woman we were on our way to meet.

"I would not go so far as to call her a courtesan, but she relies upon the kindness of strangers so to speak for part of her income. Yet strangely it seems that our Mrs Adams shuns society and keeps herself to herself for the most part, from what I can gather," Raffles remarked, whilst lighting a Sullivan. Smoke - and the fog of our breath – streamed out into the winter air.

"Did Ranji mention where he first encountered her?" I replied, pulling my coat tighter around me and nestling my chin into the woollen scarf that Lucy had recently bought for me in Truro.

"It was at a cricket event, in September. Ranji was playing in an exhibition match at Harrow, where her young son is a pupil and boarder. He met her at the reception after the game."

Raffles went on to describe how Ranji had found her "captivating". She had attracted him with her looks - but enchanted him through her conversation and wit also. Ranji hoped that his warnings about her charms would drown out any siren song Raffles might hear when they met. But it was more likely that Raffles would seduce her, I thought to myself.

Mrs Adams resided in Chiswick and we soon found ourselves passing by Turnham Green. I made reference to an excellent novel I was reading, set during the Civil War and around the Battle for Turnham Green specifically.

"There is a chance that we may have to go to battle too Bunny, should diplomacy fail. We cannot rely upon the kindness of this stranger."

I nodded in reply, resolved that we may well have to pull a job to retrieve our friend's ring. I deftly changed the subject however, not wishing to dwell upon any prospective burglary before we needed to.

"Might I ask A.J which side you would have fought on during the Civil War?"

"Why Bunny, I would have fought on whichever side you were on. My loyalty to my best friend would have eclipsed anything I owed to the Parliamentarians or the Crown. If nothing else, you would have proved far less taxing than either," Raffles replied and smiled - blending irony and affection as perfectly as any whisky and soda-water he could mix.

"I'm grateful for your loyalty, but I would be equally grateful for a serious answer – for once."

"Well just this once then I'll attempt to be serious my friend, if only to distract us both from the cold. I would have fought for the Crown – and not just because the Cavaliers were a far more romantic and amiable bunch. I find it heartening still that the most powerful man in the country – whether it be a Gladstone, Disraeli or Salisbury – has to visit the Palace each week and bow before a sage old lady, who possesses more of a sense of love and duty for this country in her little finger than our grubby politicians possess in their entire cabinets. But that's your lot Bunny, I warrant I have used up all my seriousness for the whole of the month now. Besides, we have reached our destination."

Chapter Three

As we approached the door to the three storey villa, walking through a pretty front garden to do so, I caught the sound of some beautiful singing inside, albeit I could not quite discern the precise aria. The voice was silvery, classically trained, soulful yet mournful. It was the voice of an Angel I thought to myself, or that of a Siren.

An elderly man-servant answered the door. From his rough visage – and amputated left arm – I took the servant for an ex-soldier, wounded in action. Many an injured soldier, many with no visible scars, populated London at the end of the century – having returned home from another ill-conceived foreign adventure. His mistress may well indeed be capable of kindnesses to strangers, I surmised hopefully, to show such charity and employ such a fellow.

The servant, Winwood, took our coats and led us through to the drawing room. Light filtered through Florentine blinds to illuminate an elegantly furnished room, influenced by English, American and European tastes. Portraits of both Abraham Lincoln and Ulysses S. Grant also hung next to each other in a corner by the window. The room housed a number of bookshelves, which betrayed as fine a taste in literature as furniture. I noticed works by Goethe, Stendhal, Henry and William James, Nietzsche and Tolstoy. There were shelves devoted to just plays too, by Chekhov, Racine and Sheridan, among others. Heat shimmered off the burning coals of the fireplace.

But all this detail I took in some time after first entering the drawing room. For I only had eyes for Iris Adams, I must confess, when introduced to her. To my shame I even took down the portrait of Lucy from my mind's eye temporarily – and hung in its place the searingly attractive vision of Mrs Adams. Her figure was naturally alluring – contoured rather than just fashionably slim. There was an intelligence and maturity to her manner which bespoke of a woman in her late thirties, though she appeared younger looking. Her chestnut tresses seemed spun from silk. Her hazel eyes, burnished like the richest of varnishes, glowed like the coals upon the fire. Her skin was smooth, flawless like the sheen of a pearl. There was a classicality to her beauty, yet coldness too – a fearful, as well as alluring, symmetry. She wore a white silk blouse beneath a stylish navy blue tight-fitting jacket – with equally tight-fitting trousers and boots. A small gold cross around her neck glinted in the light. Her beauty could leave a man speechless, or bumbling like an idiot. My heart throbbed as if I were in fear for my life, or in love. I drew in her beauty and breathed in her perfume, utterly and absurdly entranced. I stupidly regretted not having worn my best suit; similarly I felt acute anguish for not being as rich as a Rothschild so as to have a chance to possess such beauty. But these are just words, words, words. Akin to Shakespeare's Cleopatra, her person and beauty "beggared all description."

When I finally could bring myself to take my eyes off the politely smiling woman – each second felt like an hour – I glanced at my friend. Raffles too, it seems, was captivated.

Chapter Four

Not since Mary Flanagan had I seen Raffles look at a woman with such admiration and intrigue.

The servant introduced us, although his words were a blur in the background.

"Thank you for your note and for agreeing to see me at such short notice, Mrs Adams. This is a friend of mine, Harry Manders. I hope you do not mind him accompanying me today."

"Thank you for being so punctual, Mr Raffles. Are you the same Harry Manders who occasionally writes pieces for *The Strand* magazine?" she remarked, gazing upon me as if I were the only man in the world for her.

"I am, yes," I gladly replied, understandably stoked that she somehow knew of me.

"I enjoyed your recent piece. I do not expect that the trade union leader whom you exposed for corruption and fraud crowed much about the piece, however. Such were his proclivities towards cronyism and lying that he may well be compelled to become an MP of all things when he is removed from his current position."

I laughed, a little too enthusiastically – and fawningly.

"Please sit down, gentlemen. Would you like anything to drink? Perhaps a coffee or tea? The weather is as frosty as the reception you might receive at the next trade union gathering, Mr Manders."

I grinned, toothily, rather than laughed in response to this comment. Our hostess arranged for some tea and coffee and Winwood exited.

"Now, Mr Raffles, you must forgive me as I have agreed to see you on, partly, false pretences. I know why you wish to see me – and we will come to that manner shortly – but I must confess I principally assented to your request to call upon me because of my son's interest in cricket. Godfrey often speaks of your feats and scorecards. Would you be so kind as to sign one of his bats and a picture card he has of you?" the wondrous woman remarked, glowing as she mentioned her son. She here retrieved a new bat and a picture of Raffles from behind a chair.

"Certainly," Raffles replied. He took out his pen, signed the bat and then wrote a sentence or two. For just the briefest of moments the woman's mask of charm and composure slipped. A crack of sadness appeared in her pristine expression but she quickly returned to a vision of politeness – and loveliness – and gazed at Raffles as if he were the only man in the world for her.

Chapter Five

"I imagined that I would find you here, on behalf of Ranji, at some point Mr Raffles. Or I fancied that his other great friend, Mr Fry, would petition me on his behalf. But I should inform you that even if Dr Grace were to intercede for Ranji my response would be the same," our hostess remarked and smiled charmingly – indeed her face was even more bewitching when delivering bad news. "The ring was given to me as a gift. I did not steal it – and I intend to keep it. It will serve as a reminder to me of the brief affair. I hope that its absence will serve as a reminder to Mr Ranjitsinhji not to give his heart, or valuables, away so freely."

There was now steel behind the silk of her voice. Iris Adams became as imperious, as well as beautiful, as Cleopatra.

"Mrs Adams, I can sympathise with your position. But permit me to speak, briefly. When I spoke to Ranji, please know that I did not pry into the intimacies of your relationship. I will also not beg you now for your side of the story in regards to the affair. I just want you to understand that Ranji is one of the most decent fellows I know – and if he hurt you then it was more from carelessness that wilful malice. As you may already know the ring possesses a certain ceremonial, as well as monetary, value. I believe that Ranji has already made you a generous offer to buy back the ring. Ranji is unaware of this but I also have a cheque in my pocket, from me, made out to the same amount to add to his offer. I would ask you to re-consider, Mrs Adams."

There was silk to Raffles' steel. He was charming as well as determined. Few women could resist my friend – but Iris Adams was unlike few women he had ever encountered.

"You are a good friend it seems Mr Raffles, but I have no desire to take your money or that of Mr Ranjitsinhji. Indeed, perhaps more than a monetary or ceremonial value, you will now appreciate the educational value the ring holds. Not only will my actions teach your friend to be less, as you say, careless in the future – but so too both of you should learn the important lesson that it is not now the province of women to just serve the will and demands of men. Ranji was more than just a little careless too when we parted, he was unkind. He grew resentful when I conveyed to him that our relationship could never be more than what it was. I loved my first husband dearly and I shall never re-marry Mr Raffles. But that was not all. Ranji also grew jealous when he discovered that he had a rival for my affections and attention."

It was here that Raffles gave the pre-arranged signal. He merely gently drummed his fingers upon the arm of the leather chair he was sat upon.

Chapter Six

The signal meant that it was time to remove myself from the room, employing the excuse of asking to use the bathroom. Winwood here entered with a tray of tea, coffee and cakes and pointed me upstairs. As Raffles had discussed that morning, my task was to search all relevant rooms for the ring (albeit we knew the unlikelihood of finding it out in the open), or a safe. Also, armed with a supply of wax, I was to make an impression of any keys I found. Suffice to say I felt more than a little uneasy at snooping around the house, but my determination to assist Raffles and Ranji bested my discomfort and fear. The perfume pervading her bedroom assaulted my senses – and I blushed as I went through her drawers – but I hastily made impressions of the keys I located and completed my mission. Such was my nervous state afterwards that, ironically, I did need to use the bathroom before I ventured back downstairs.

As I re-entered the room, attempting to appear as relaxed as possible (although my heart was beating as much as if our hostess had just invited me up to her bedroom for a different reason), I caught Raffles and Mrs Adams trading quotes from Shakespeare.

They seemed to be bickering, or flirting, like Beatrice and Benedick.

"To be wise and love exceeds man's might," Raffles exclaimed, quoting from *Troilus and Cressida* - no doubt trying to apologise for Ranji's behaviour.

"Give me that man that is not passion's slave, and I will wear him in my heart's core," she replied, quoting from *Hamlet*.

Raffles thanked her for the tea and she thanked him for kindly signing her son's cricket bat and pictures. Although still at odds over the issue of the ring, we mentioned it not and were the soul of politeness. Raffles got up and walked around the room, commenting upon some of the paintings. As he did so I found myself giving in to curiosity and picking up and reading the inscription Raffles had written upon his picture. I recognised that the lines were from A. E. Housman.

"For Godfrey,
Now in Maytime to the wicket
Out I march with bat and pad:
See the son of grief at cricket
Trying to be glad."

Finally we took our leave.

"You should come to the house again sometime, Mr Raffles."

"I will do soon Mrs Adams, I promise."

"Perhaps you could visit when Godfrey is home for the holidays. He could pester you about cricket, and I could pester you about

Shakespeare," she remarked solicitously. She invited me too – with the invitation being the very soul of an afterthought.

Despite our mission having failed Raffles was radiating with delight as we left the house and strode towards Turnham Green, where we hoped to flag down a cab.

"What did you think of her?" I asked, more curious than usual as to Raffles' views upon a subject.

"She is a lovely woman, with a face that a man might die for," he replied, grinning - as much to himself as me. I began to worry that Iris Adams might seduce the greatest spin bowler of our generation, as well as its greatest batsman.

Pleased with my success at locating and making an impression of so many keys, Raffles promised to buy me dinner later that evening. He took the various wax impressions from me and said he would pass them on to a key cutting contact he had. The keys would be ready by tomorrow afternoon.

"So are we going to do the job tomorrow night?" I asked, oscillating between those two familiar bedfellows of excitement and fear.

"Well I did promise to visit the house again soon – and one should always keep a promise to a lady, old chap."

Raffles said little else during our cab ride home. He merely sat there, ash hanging off barely-smoked cigarettes – a charming smile lining his handsome features. The expression was akin to the one I often wore whilst day-dreaming about Lucy, I fancied.

I spent the remainder of the afternoon catching up on some work. I had been commissioned to write a piece about the ever fractious divide in the Tory Party about its stance towards Europe – and how isolationist or integrated we should be. Perhaps thinking of the portrait of Abraham Lincoln in Iris Adams' drawing room I commented that, "A house divided against itself cannot stand." Thinking of Shakespeare however, I concluded by wishing for "a plague on both their houses!"

Chapter Seven

We ran into Thomas "Arrows" Fletcher, a journalist friend of mine, at Boodles and asked him to join us for dinner. The company was as enjoyable as the food (I had the salmon and game pie). The conversation flowed, as did the champagne which Raffles ordered. He requested that he keep the corks from all the bottles we ordered. His explanation was that his eccentric uncle collected them. We all had uncles with far greater eccentricities, and no one batted an eyelid as to the request. I could not help but smile into my napkin though, knowing the real reason behind Raffles' strange request.

Once ensconced back at the Albany, cradling a brandy which was as warming as the fire, I brought up the subject of our imminent job. Firstly, I asked if Raffles could even be sure that the ring was still in the lady's possession and at the house, as opposed to stored in a safe deposit box at her bank, or with her lawyer.

"There is that double possibility. But I am inclined to think neither. Women are naturally secretive, and they like to do their own secreting. Why should she hand it over to anyone else?"

Raffles replied, again gently smiling in a playful fashion. I briefly thought how I had perhaps heard someone say something similar before, or had read something similar in a book.

"But even if the woman has kept the ring, would she not have placed such an item in her own safe? And where –"

"It's located behind the portrait of Ulysses Grant. I was not admiring the decor earlier today Bunny when I went around the room, which is not to say that our hostess did not possess an admirable sense of taste. But my purpose was to find a secret panel, or safe. I just hope that the key to the strong box I saw behind the painting was located in plain sight in her bedroom – else Ranji's odds of recovering his ring might become as long as Trumper scoring a pair."

Perhaps I was becoming used to Raffles astounding me, or maybe I was tired, but I reacted with little surprise to his revealing the location of the safe. Also, we had a long way to go before we could raise our glasses of brandy in a toast, celebrating success. Rather I raised mine to my mouth, fearing failure.

During another drink or two Raffles went over the plan again for the following evening. We would meet at his rooms just off the King's Rd, where we would pick up the tools of our trade and put on some suitable attire.

"Not only must we blend in with the night, but perhaps more importantly, black never goes out of style," Raffles remarked, perhaps only half jokingly.

Chapter Eight

Charcoal grey clouds smudged an already inky firmament. Thankfully the moon was as slender as Iris Adams' figure as we approached her house in the dead of night. Even the badgers and the barmen at Boodles would be asleep by now. Raffles removed a number of champagne corks from his coat and placed them on top of the spikes upon the garden railings. We then placed our coats over the corks and climbed over onto the property with ease. I briefly raised my eyes to the heavens – and whispered a fleeting prayer – that one of the keys we cut was a fit for the Chubb lock on the front door. Raffles had brought along a number of skeleton keys to combat that lock should we be out of luck, but they proved surplus to requirements.

"Well done, Bunny," Raffles whispered enthusiastically as he opened the door. The compliment warmed my heart more than any fire - or brandy even.

The lingering fragrance of the unnervingly attractive woman assaulted my senses (again) as we entered the drawing room. Again I suffered a slight crisis of conscience, that we were perhaps wronging such a paragon of beauty. Although one could argue

Iris Adams was not exactly a paragon of virtue, I could conversely argue that no one was. I recalled the quote from Dostoyevsky, that "Beauty will save the world." Yet could not the aspiration to possess such beauty equally damn the world, debase rather than inspire? Iris Adams was perhaps more of a Calypso or Circe than Penelope. In the dead of night her countenance burned even brighter. My inward eye had been branded by her image. My hand gripped the handle of the carpet bag, which contained the tools of our trade – and I recalled my loyalty towards Ranji to help stiffen my resolve. I wondered, would Lucy's mettle even be attractive enough to save me should Iris Adams seduce me?

"Bunny, Bunny," Raffles whispered, this time with a harshness more than enthusiasm. I was duly jolted out of my ill-timed reverie. "Pass me the bag. Also, unlock the window. Should we be disturbed it'll be our best escape route. We should be able to hear that lead-footed Winwood from a mile off."

First checking for any wires that could have been attached to an alarm, Raffles carefully removed the painting of General Grant. Even Raffles here muttered a prayer I suspect that one of the keys we had cut was the right one to the strong box which was encased in the wall. The sound of the click of the lock turning over was as welcome as that of the clink of ice into a glass to signal the first gin and tonic for the day. We shared both a sigh and relief and triumphant smile as Raffles reached into the safe and pulled out a ring case. When I took in the ruby, glowing akin to a heart throbbing, I could understand why the woman did not want to part from such gem. As well as extracting the ring from the safe I also noticed Raffles place a large envelope in the strong box, before re-locking it.

I was just about to enquire as to what Raffles had left in the safe when I was interrupted by the increasingly familiar – and always alarming – sound of a revolver being cocked.

We had been caught out.

Chapter Nine

A silk, shimmering scarlet night gown clung to an hour glass figure. A triangle of flesh glistened beneath her neck. Her hair hung down, un-styled but yet not ill-styled. Iris Adams stood before us, feline yet masterful. Her beauty transfixed me as much as the revolver, which she handled with familiarity and purpose. Raffles smiled politely, seemingly unmoved by her beauty or the weapon, and bowed his head slightly as if he were merely meeting the woman again at a garden party.

"The best that you can hope for is that you are imprisoned and your reputation is ruined. The worst is that you are shot, with our without impunity, as an intruder. Yet given your reputation and standing in society, perhaps the best fate to befall you will be that I shoot you - and you will be unable to see your name upon the front, rather than back, pages of the newspapers. You will be revealed and reviled as an amateur cracksman — a very amateur cracksman, given that you have been apprehended during your first job."

If only I had had a napkin to smile behind in regards to this comment. There was little else to smile about however. We were done for. I had a brief vision of the headlines – and myself standing in the dock. Not even Thomas "Arrows" Fletcher would give us a favourable write up in regards to the trial.

"Will you allow a condemned man one last cigarette?" Raffles asked, as he removed his silver cigarette case (a gift from Ranji) and lit a Sullivan.

"You seem remarkably calm, Mr Raffles. Either you are a great actor, or the very soul of indifference."

"I may well be both, but on this occasion I fancy that I am neither," Raffles replied. Smoked curled upwards, as did the corners of his mouth, in a knowing (but not self-satisfied) smile.

"Do you think that I will not turn you over to the police, or use this gun? You should not underestimate me. A great man once did before, but I bettered even him in the end."

"I do not underestimate you, believe me. But I do not believe that you will turn me over to the police."

"And give me one good reason why I shouldn't give you up, Mr Raffles?"

"Because I did not give you up, Mrs Irene Norton, née Adler."

Chapter Ten

My eyes widened at the revelation (which again Raffles had typically kept me in the dark about). I also believe I let out a gasp. Irene Adler. "*The* woman," as Sherlock Holmes had called her, who had bested him during the episode reported in *A Scandal in Bohemia*. Dr Watson's account had made "*the* woman" famous, or infamous, since its publication – albeit the former opera singer and actress had exited the stage after marrying Godfrey Norton. She had disappeared. She was more legend than flesh and blood, in some respects. Yet she stood before us now, as much a legend as flesh and blood. Age had not withered her.

Irene Adler at first lowered the gun, but then raised it again – and clasped the handle tighter, as if we were an even greater threat to her well being.

"How did you know?"

"If I were Sherlock Holmes I could say that my suspicions were raised in hearing your accent and observing the decor, the mixture of European and American influences. I also asked myself, why would such a beautiful, accomplished woman – who could turn herself into a social lioness in any capital of the world – choose to shun society? Why was she hiding herself away? Such is your knowledge of Shakespeare that I fancied you were an actress at some point – and Bunny and I were fortunate enough to hear your classically trained singing voice just before we first met you yesterday. Your son Godfrey is named after his father too, no? Aye, if I were Sherlock Holmes these things would have added up to something and I would have deduced the truth. But, in truth, I had front row seats to a performance of *Othello* you acted in on the continent many years ago – and I recognised you."

"Yet you did not use my secret against me? I value my privacy over any piece of jewellery. You could have blackmailed me, or turned me over to certain authorities. Mr Holmes was kind in his assessment of my character, but you are doubtless aware that I have not led a wholly blameless life. My reputation, like my cooking, is not to be envied," she replied, whilst lowering the gun and raising a smile.

"To quote your former President, hanging up on the wall behind me, "Character is like a tree and reputation like a shadow. The shadow is what we think of it; the tree is the real thing." Besides, blackmail isn't my style."

"But burglary is?" the woman remarked, with laughter then blooming out, as musical and beautiful as any aria. Raffles and I laughed too, albeit the joke we shared was different. There is many a true word spoken in jest.

"It seems that you weren't that surprised to find us here. Indeed, you were almost expecting us. Can I ask – how did you know?" Raffles asked.

"You did not strike me as someone who would give up his wicket, or his friend, easily. Also, Mr Manders left a few telling pieces of wax stuck to my keys."

"Well done, Bunny," was all my companion said in regards to my error.

"Suffice to say you have caught us out Mrs Adams – and you may serve us up our just desserts. But no matter what, rest assured I will keep my word and not reveal your secret. You have a right to your privacy and to write a new chapter into your life."

"Call me Irene. And, to quote my former President behind you, "I have always found that mercy bears richer fruit than strict justice." You may give the ring back to Ranji. Although I would you advise him that when he next gives it away, it should be to someone who he believes should keep it."

Chapter Eleven

We were soon sitting down to tea and cakes again, with the woman who we had set out to rob that evening. Irene Adler spoke about the loss of her husband and how she wanted to bring up her son in England. For both her own sake – and for the sake of her son – she had changed her name. She just wished to play the role of a good mother. She missed her husband, but enjoyed her own company and kept herself occupied. She regretted having few friends in London though and invited Raffles to call upon her later in the week (I had been relegated to something less than an afterthought by now I warrant). In reply to this invitation however Raffles half-jokingly explained that it might not prove to be a good idea.

"One of us may end up seducing the other, unwittingly or not. And neither of us would want that."

There's many a true word spoken in jest.

Raffles did promise though that he would give a talk to her son's year at Harrow – and try to arrange a cricket match there during the summer. It was perhaps due to her realising that she may not see Raffles again that Irene Adler said the following. She stood in the doorway, the morning rays of the sun stretching out to touch an equally bright star.

"I met her once, Raffles. She was a lovely woman. I know that what you wrote for Godfrey applies even more so to you."

We stood in the garden. Winwood was unlocking the gate. I should have assisted him, given his one arm, but I could not help but observe this final exchange between Raffles and Irene Adler. He looked at her, far more caught out here than when she had held a gun to him the night before. I had no idea who this "lovely woman" was. A brief grateful smile succeeded his haunted, pained expression.

"Thank you."

Whilst walking towards Turnham Green, in order to hail a cab, I asked Raffles what had been in the envelope that he had placed in the safe after extracting the ring. He answered that he had written the woman a letter, explaining certain things that he had been able to ultimately tell her in person. The envelope also contained a sum of money, from Ranji and himself, which he hoped would compensate her for the loss of the ring. School fees don't pay themselves, he posited.

Our journey back to central London passed in silence. The morning was bright, but I sensed an old familiar gloom begin to hang over my friend. He soon slept, or pretended to be asleep. Despite the evening's revelation of meeting Irene Adler I could not help but dwell upon Raffles – and the look upon his face during her final words to him. I could count on one hand the amount of times I had witnessed someone shock or depress my friend with something they had said, or done. Fearing I may never be permitted another opportunity again I brought the subject up as the cab dropped me off at my apartment and we were saying our farewells.

"I hope you do not mind me asking A. J. – but who is the woman to whom Irene referred earlier?"

There was a kindness as well as sadness in his features whilst he paused, before replying.

"*The* woman. Now as I've used up my quota of seriousness for the month Bunny that's all I will say on the matter. Get some sleep old chap – and when you wake up write to Lucy. Tell her how much she means to you."

And with that he signalled the cabman to ride on. I heeded Raffles' advice and when I got up to my rooms I caught up on some sleep. It was whilst composing a note to Lucy when I woke that I received a letter from her, telling me how much I meant to her – and I realised that she was indeed mettle more attractive than Irene Adler.

I smiled.

RAFFLES:

STUMPED

Chapter One

"Now Bunny, I am hoping that you have had a sufficient amount to drink to finally tell me what's on your mind. You chewed your nails and bottom lip more than your fillet mignon at dinner. You are also still looking like a man whose funeral – or worse, wedding – is tomorrow," Raffles exclaimed whilst loosening his tie and topping us both up.

We were working our way through a fine bottle of Madeira back at Raffles' apartment at the Albany, after dinner at the Savile Club. It was a month or so before our encounter with Sherlock Holmes (the events of which can be found in *Raffles: The Gentleman Thief*). A summer breeze wafted through the window and cooled my flushed features.

"I am sorry A.J if I have been poor company this evening. But there's the rub. I am poor. Indeed to be poverty stricken may even prove to be an aspiration right now, for I am in a far more perilous state. I am debt ridden."

I went on to explain how, despite my "work" with Raffles over the past few months (as a cracksman's accomplice), I had still not wholly freed myself from my financial straits. My present predicament stemmed from owing a significant amount of capital to a moneylender called Alexander Cardinal. Cardinal revelled in his nickname of Shylock. He specialised in targeting gentlemen of leisure. I was befriended by one of his agents in a casino one evening, who introduced me to his well dressed, well spoken employer at Cardinal's house in Notting Hill. I borrowed a sum of money from him to pay, at a reasonable rate of interest, certain other debts. He called it a "quick quid" to help tide things over. Although we signed a contract, we also had a gentleman's agreement that I would pay off the loan – and interest – when certain investments I owned matured. These investments were gilt-edged and served as my security.

"Yet I found out this week that Cardinal is no gentleman. He has proved a fiend rather than friend. Employing a technical clause in the contract he is calling in the debt, or else he will be upping the rate of interest during the interim period before I can collect on my investments. I am to meet with him the day after tomorrow. If I do not have his money - which I don't - then he says he will seek to destroy my reputation by informing my family and employers of my indebtedness. Cardinal also employs a number of thugs who will look to inflict harm upon my body, rather than my good name. I am caught between Scylla and Charybdis, Raffles. My lack of funds has only been matched by my lack of sleep over the last day or so. I fear I will just have to relinquish all my investments to him – and thus leave me ruined for years to come."

Raffles opened his silver cigarette case and handed me a Sullivan. His face had betrayed neither sympathy nor indifference when listening to my plight.

"You have a trusting nature, Bunny. 'Tis a virtue I admire old chap, as is your trustworthiness, but others see such virtues as weaknesses rather than strengths. I have heard about this Alexander Cardinal. He is as rapacious as he is niggarding, I understand. He is also a hermit somewhat, or agoraphobic is the term I believe, hence he conducts his business dealings at home. He lives with just his manservant, a former soldier, who also serves as his minder."

"And he has heard of you Raffles in return, it seems. When he discovered that you were an acquaintance he spoke of a passion for cricket and a desire to meet you. I duly played down our friendship, as I did not wish for him to have any thoughts of ensnaring you also. I will not have you in his debt too and suffer my fate."

My friend stood up and commenced to pace around the room - his head bowed, deep in thought. After two laps around his armchair and desk he finally stopped, lifted his head and smiled.

"You must ask Cardinal to pay me a visit here, upon the evening after tomorrow. Let us say 9.00. You should state, to further entice the fox from his burrow at such an hour, that you will pay the debt in full. And you will be paying off your debt with your very own hard earned money, Bunny."

"But how? Raffles, you are being absurd. A whole year's earnings from my writing would be needed to pay off the sum. And if you are thinking that we could pull a job in that time then it's out of the question. We would need time to locate and reconnaissance the place. Also, we would need the house to be empty – and for there to be enough boodle about. No, I will not permit you to risk your neck, or for there to be any blood spilled," I vehemently exclaimed.

"Bunny, I need you to utilise your trusting nature one last time – by trusting me."

I smiled, feebly, and nodded my head but I was stumped if I knew how Raffles thought he could deliver me from my ruinous fate within forty eight hours.

Chapter Two

The Madeira may have wiped away some of my brain cells, but alas it did not wipe away my debts when I awoke the next morning. As I had promised Raffles my task for the day was to visit my persecutor. Cardinal's house – and his intimidating character – loomed large in my mind but I confronted them both that afternoon.

Perhaps a certain desperation of having nothing left to lose, or my growing resentment for the odious usurer, emboldened me to hold fast in my insistence that Raffles would meet with Cardinal – but only in the evening and at the Albany. It rankled with his pride - and the prospect of venturing outdoors discomforted him - but Cardinal agreed to the meeting. He explained how he was keen to meet the famous cricketer who could "turn a game with the turn of his wrist." And of course he was eager to have me settle my debt with him, one way or another.

"I'll either have the money, or you, in my pocket by the end of the week Mr Manders," Cardinal remarked with self-satisfaction – and then cackled to himself. I looked up to see his smarmy butler-soldier grinning too. I was a source of amusement, as well as revenue, to the broker of the "quick quid" it seemed.

Later that evening Raffles insisted that I join him for a function at Lord's. He briefly went over the arrangements for the following night during the cab journey over to the hallowed ground. I was to bring my spare key to the Albany as Raffles was due to run an errand and he might be late for the meeting.

"However tardy I might be though you must keep the villain at the Albany. State that I will be bringing his money along. Mention too how I am keen to meet him, to discuss cricket or business opportunities. Just keep the predator in your sights, Bunny. I will look after everything else."

Chapter Three

I woke early the following day, the sunlight screeching through my window, but in a gesture towards not wishing to face the day ahead I remained in bed, Oblomov-like, for some time. I tried to read but not even Tennyson – or Pope – could distract me from my black thoughts. If I could just awake tomorrow free from the clutches of my Shylock then I promised myself that I would be as prudent with my money as George Peabody. There are no "quick quids", just hard times. One cannot lift oneself out of debt by borrowing and digging a bigger hole for oneself.

"Come what may, time and the hour run through the roughest day," I told myself, unconvincingly. I prayed to God that things would work out and that I would escape ruination – but in many ways, more than God, I was praying to Raffles.

I must confess that I was less assured that God might answer my prayers when Raffles failed to answer his door. As instructed though I had brought the spare key and I let myself in. Cardinal arrived on the hour. One could have put his age at fifty, or seventy. Light shone off his silvery grey hair and balding head. Beady, hazel eyes shone out behind serpent-like eye-lids. His face was long, cheeks sunken akin to a cadaver's and his black expression – and black garb – gave him the air of an undertaker. Aye, in some ways he was here for my funeral, I thought to myself. The moneylender was accompanied by his manservant cum bodyguard, Gough. Gough (he had neither a Christian name nor Christian bone in his body) stood six feet tall. A long pink scar marked the side of his flame-haired head from where a bullet had grazed him during the battle of Maiwand. A scowl marked Gough's appearance too when he entered the apartment. As transfixed as one could be by his broken nose and cauliflower ears I could not help notice the bulge in his jacket also, where he kept his revolver.

"Where's our host?" Cardinal asked, already in a state of impatience and displeasure.

"I am afraid that Raffles is running late. Can I fix you both a drink while we wait?" I replied, whilst already pouring a large gin and tonic for myself.

"No. I wish to keep a clear head. And Gough does not drink whilst on duty."

Although the ex-soldier remained stone-faced, sentry-like, I sensed a flicker of disappointment still in his expression.

"So this is the Albany?" Cardinal exclaimed, arching his eyebrow and surveying the tastefully furnished apartment. "Your friend Raffles must have a private income, for surely he cannot make any significant sums of money from playing cricket? Although I hope to change that by making him an offer he can't refuse. Perhaps I shall have both of you in my pocket by the end of the evening," the moneylender remarked and smirked, a dog-tooth poking out from beneath his top lip as he did so.

I took another swig of my gin and tonic, draining the glass, with the contents of Cardinal's - and Gough's - pockets worrying me equally, but for different reasons.

Chapter Four

"I am most displeased, Mr Manders. Time is money - a lesson which you will learn all the more if you are unable to settle your debt this evening."

It was an hour or so since Cardinal had first arrived. Raffles was still absent. He now needed to turn up with some tonic water, as well as Cardinal's pound of flesh. I had apologised repeatedly, with Gough grunting in disdain each time I did so. Yet, as per instructed by Raffles, I held fast and persuaded his guests to stay.

"And if you bide your time and remain a little longer Mr Cardinal, you shall have your money," I replied, with perhaps more conviction in my voice than in my heart.

"I just hope that Mr Raffles' timing with his bat upon the field is better than his punctuality off it."

Another half an hour or so passed. Cardinal often sighed, rolled his eyes and checked his watch. Sometimes he paced around the room and examined certain pieces of furniture and paintings, or he sat stern-faced in a chair by the fire – like a judge about to deliver the death penalty. Gough cracked his knuckles and glared at me too – licking his lips smirking, as if he were a hangman about to carry out the judge's sentence.

"This is intolerable. It seems that your friend has abandoned you," Cardinal posited, looking at his watch once more.

"Never," I replied, with perhaps more conviction in my heart than in my voice.

"Thank you for keeping faith Bunny, and for keeping our guests entertained until my arrival." Raffles had entered many a different residence before in silence, so it was unsurprising that he could enter his own apartment unnoticed too. "I apologise, Mr Cardinal, for my tardiness. And I hope that I haven't put your nose out of joint too, Sir, even more so than it already seems to be," Raffles remarked when turning to Gough. The surly ex-soldier flared his nostrils and screwed up his face, offended, but Raffles ignored the fellow and lit a Sullivan. Cardinal raised a hand to his minder, which served to tame him.

"I will not say that I have been overly content to wait this long Mr Raffles, but I am pleased that you have finally graced us with your presence."

"Bunny tells me that you are a cricket fan, Mr Cardinal. You must let me apologise in deeds, rather than just words, and offer you and your associate a couple of tickets to the next Gentlemen versus Players match," Raffles politely expressed, whilst fixing himself a whisky and soda-water.

"Your offer is kind, but unnecessary. Our time will now be brief this evening so I should come to the point. My interest in cricket, I should confess to you Mr Raffles, derives from my interest in making money. I am here tonight in order to represent a consortium of gentlemen who like to, shall we say, even the odds when deciding the outcome of a cricket match. You would make a valuable addition to our team of players. Most players join our ranks because, like Mr Manders here, they fall into debt and need a helping hand. Yet any money you make from us will be pure profit. Imagine, even when you lose a game of cricket, you could still be a winner in a financial sense."

Cardinal's whole face here smiled – his mouth and serpentine eyes. The wrinkles in his brow were also smoothed out.

I knew, more so than anyone, how Raffles was not immune from making a dishonest quick quid and I imagine that he was tempted by the devil's offer – but Raffles was Raffles. He shook his head, as if bored or pitying the moneylender, and replied,

"When the One Great Scorer comes
To write against your name,
He marks – not that you won or lost –
But how you played the game."

The smile fell from the villain's face as surely as if Raffles had just bowled him out. Indeed his smile turned into a grimace – but then Cardinal regained his composure. I dare say that few of the players in his team of match fixers had sold their souls so quickly – and the scout did not want to give up signing up such a prized player without giving him a second chance.

"It would be unwise to say no now my friend, without giving the matter some serious thought. You could be saying goodbye to a lot of money by saying goodbye to my associates and I without a fair hearing."

"Money lost, little lost. Honour lost, much lost," Raffles calmly replied, with silk and steel in his tone. "And I would thank you, Mr Cardinal, for not calling me your friend. My friend is sitting opposite you – and I can assure you that you and he are quite unalike."

The aged moneylender pursed his lips and his bony fingers gripped the arms of the leather chair like talons – but he finally smiled, twistedly, and responded.

"Mr Manders may well be quite unlike me Mr Raffles, as you say, but we are tied together through a bond as strong – if not stronger – than friendship. That of a financial bond. And I'll have my bond; speak not against my bond," Cardinal remarked with dramatic relish, quoting his namesake, Shylock.

"Will you not reconsider your position and revert to the original terms of your agreement with Bunny? His investments will mature soon and you will have your money."

"I have the contract with me, but at no point does it include a clause in which a dandified cricketer can alter the terms of the agreement. 'Tis not in the bond. And I'll have my bond," the usurer exclaimed, with glee and animus lacing his tone. "You think I but crave my money, but what I am merely looking for is justice. Isn't that right, Gough?"

"That's right, Mr Cardinal," Gough chipped in, cracking his knuckles again and toothily grinning (to reveal a lack of front teeth).

"Though justice be thy plea, consider this: that in the course of justice none of us should see salvation," Raffles pronounced, quoting from *The Merchant of Venice* also.

"It seems that you only have fine words to offer up, rather than actual money," Cardinal drily posited.

Raffles shook his head, either in pity for the moneylender - or in disappointment, that he could not save me from financial ruin.

"You may dress like a gentleman Mr Cardinal, but the apparel does not always proclaim the man it seems."

"A.J, it's fine if you have not been able to raise the capital. I am grateful for your help, but it was not your problem to solve," I said disconsolately, trying my best to console my friend.

"I have drawn up some new terms, which will extend the deadline for when you can repay your debt. I will grant you some additional time. But as I mentioned earlier in the evening Mr Manders, time is money. If you would just read over and sign the new contract."

Raffles and I glanced at each other, but there would be no last minute reprieve. Yet I was heartened by the fact that, though I would lose my assets, I would not lose my friend. Gough retrieved some papers from his pocket and handed them to Cardinal, who tickled the air with his fingers in anticipation of receiving them before placing the contract on the table by his chair.

"Here, use my pen, old chap. Also, if you need some paper to blot the ink with use this," Raffles said, whilst removing a five pound note from his inside pocket and handing it to me. "Or this, or this, or this, or this, or this, or this. Indeed, I do believe that I have enough blotting paper here, Bunny, to absorb all of your debts."

My prayers had been answered.

Chapter Five

Cardinal was aghast – and banged his tight, bony first upon the table, causing the contract to fall upon the carpet.

"What is this mockery?" he loudly croaked, spittle falling upon the carpet, too.

"Justice," Raffles wryly replied whilst still retrieving money from his pocket, as it were a magical font for the stuff.

"You have made a fool out of me."

"We both know that you have made a fool out of yourself, Mr Cardinal."

Gough here grunted, or snorted, and moved towards Raffles, but Cardinal raised his hand again. Justice, or the law, would not be on his side if he were responsible for assaulting a gentleman in the Albany. It was not in the bond. Our Shylock merely proceeded to count the money, twice, before leaving. He did so in silence. Gough however pronounced the following, as he stood at the door.

"Maybe we'll bump into each other again someday, Mr Raffles."

"I look forward to it. Note that you may need to change your tailor though should you wish to get in and encounter me at one of my clubs," Raffles smilingly countered, riling the brute even more.

It was only when my former tormenters exited – and I locked the door behind them – that I finally sighed with relief. Raffles and I then laughed, albeit for what exact reason I knew not. I clasped my friend heartily by the hand and thanked him, tears welling in my eyes – before finally giving in to my emotions, for once, and embracing him. It was only when we were sat by the fireplace, whisky and soda-waters in hand, that I finally asked,

"How did you do it? Where did the money come from? I promise to pay you back A.J – and with interest, should you desire it."

"There's no need to pay me back. As I told you before old chap, you would be paying off your debt with your own hard earned money. Well, maybe I was exaggerating about the hard earned bit. Perhaps we should say, well earned."

"But I'm stumped. What money have I earned?"

"The money from our job this evening. You were right the other night, Bunny. We needed a target that was wealthy – and whose house would be empty. Some people rob Peter to pay Paul. We robbed an Alexander, in order to pay Alexander."

My eyes widened in shock, but then in mirth. Things fell into place, like a tumbler lock within a safe.

"I had to meet the fence directly afterwards – and recognising my desperation he robbed us on the price for our boodle – but your half of the haul more than covered your debts, old chap. So, cheers."

"To a cardinal crime," I added, as we clinked glasses.

"Now for that you should be punished, Bunny."

"You do not think that he will suspect foul play on our part?"

"I am a dandified cricketer Bunny, who is wealthy enough to turn down a bribe to fix a match. I suspect that I will be beyond suspicion. No, the list of potential culprits will run as long as his account books. I dare say, as a result of this night, the old miser will be even more disinclined to venture outside."

"Raffles. You are the man who can turn someone's fortunes at the turn of a lock. I feel I will be forever in your debt however. Thank you."

"You have no need to thank me old chap, it was my pleasure. Besides, more than you thanking me, I should be apologising to you."

"How so?"

"Mea culpa. I ran out of tonic water."

RAFFLES:

PLAYING ON

Chapter One

I spent Christmas with Raffles - which is an episode worthy of its own story, about which I may write one day - and although we had planned to spend New Year together I received a message on the morning of December 29th informing me that my friend had decided to take a trip abroad. Raffles' departure was as sudden as it was mysterious – and I was not a little aggrieved that he had left in such an abrupt manner, without saying goodbye in person. Worry soon replaced any grievance however upon reading in the newspaper how the notorious criminal Jack Shanks had escaped from prison. Our encounter with Shanks can be found in *Raffles: A Perfect Wicket.* The episode had ended with the famous (though not entirely brilliant) Inspector Lestrade of Scotland Yard apprehending Shanks, with Raffles having played an integral part in his capture. My worry was that the villain was out for revenge. Perhaps Raffles had shared my anxieties – which would have explained his hasty departure. My fears were heightened when the newspaper ran a report of Shanks being sighted in Paris (the same week that Raffles had sent me a postcard from the French capital).

Weeks passed into months, but still my friend returned not to London. I received the occasional letter. Raffles wrote to me from Copenhagen, saying that he was intending to write a short biography of the philosopher Soren Kierkegaard. Yet a fortnight later he was in Vienna, reportedly having an affair with an Austrian ballerina. When I visited the likes of the Savile Club and Boodles I was often questioned as to Raffles' whereabouts, to which I often had to confess my ignorance. Equally gossip-mongers would come up to me to share their explanations as to my friend's absence. The Australian cricket association had asked him to gain Australian citizenship and play for them, in order to help win back the Ashes. Risible. He was in Rome, helping to coach a team of priests from the Vatican, whose mission was to tour Abyssinia and civilise the country through the word of God – and cricket. Laughable. He was in Berlin, operating as a spy. Possible.

Whether they were a welcome distraction or not, my own anxieties grew to eclipse those I owned for Raffles throughout those winter and spring months. During that time I continued to court Lucy Rosebery. Sometimes we would write to each other two or three times a day, about everything and nothing. We also regularly saw each other. I travelled down on the train to Truro and at least once a month Lucy would come up to London. The day was less of a day if somehow I did not hear from her. I would leave her perfumed letters on my desk, just to breathe in her scent whilst I worked. I felt confident and comfortable in her company. She made me laugh, both at myself and the world. Every time

I saw Lucy I noticed something new about her, which only heightened her beauty and intelligence. Although I must confess I considered Lucy intelligent despite – rather than because – of her devotion to the suffragette cause. I was far less enamoured with the cause after being introduced to the sorority of zealots in person. It is the working classes who am I a feared for most, should they be granted the vote. Not only are they determined not to then allow working class women the vote, but chief among their causes once enfranchised will be to save the working classes via temperance from alcohol. I suspect the working classes will feel damned, rather than saved, should the middle classes try to edify them further. Lucy is the only suffragette I have ever seen laugh or smile - indeed they may well tax those two indulgences, along with alcohol, should they win the vote.

But forgive my digressing. My anxieties stemmed not from Lucy, but rather her father, Prescott Rosebery. How could so fair a woman be the daughter of someone so foul?

Chapter Two

"I am curious to know which will diminish first, my daughter's interest in you or your bank account - as you try to court her on a hack's salary," Prescott Rosebery exclaimed with a snigger, when we were alone together during my second trip down to Truro. He was of that new moneyed class which takes great pleasure in seeing the demise of the old moneyed class. He regularly cited Darwin and eugenics to explain how the merchant class were the new demi-gods. "We have bigger heads, bigger brains." I could certainly bear witness to his first assertion.

"Whilst you were at your fancy school, Manders, reading your Shakespeare and Cicero, I was out in the real world, or reading about J. P. Morgan or Rockefeller... The rich don't need to inherit the earth Manders, we already own it."

Should you have looked at Prescott Rosebery you may have concluded that he was more of the school of thought of the survival of the fattest, as opposed to fittest, such was his pot-belly and barrel-shaped face. He wore a signet ring upon one of his gherkin-shaped fingers that, although engraved with a crest, was about as old as the pair of cufflinks I had bought for myself at Christmas. He was forever harping on about how the House of Lords needed reforming, in hope of being able to pay his way into the chamber. He resented the aristocratic classes, for he knew he could never be truly part of their world, no matter how much money he had in the bank. He was aware, albeit he would never admit it, that he lacked sufficient intelligence and taste.

Despite her "fashionable" – and "unfashionable" – opinions, Lucy was the apple of her father's eye however. He permitted our relationship, but at no point hinted that he would allow us to become engaged. To him I was a plaything for her, until he could introduce her to a suitable demi-god of capitalism. I dare say I also amused him, like a worm wriggling upon a hook, as I squirmed and tried to win his respect – in order to win the hand of his daughter. He would often stick pins in me, belittling my profession or the amount of money I earned, in front of Lucy. She would often act as if her father were merely joking in such circumstances. Or she would try and defend him, arguing that he was used to having his own way – as though this should be a justification for him continuing to behave like a bully.

As much as my heart would lift every time I saw Lucy, it would duly sink in the presence of her odious father. Even with my additional income from my exploits with Raffles, I knew that I would never have enough money – or "be good enough" – to secure Lucy's hand in marriage. And, despite her love for me, I knew that Lucy would never defy her father and elope (the unspoken truth was that she was worried about him carrying out his threat to cut her off from any inheritance should she displease him in a particular way). I found myself offering up small prayers to heaven every time he sneezed or winced in pain from gout. Yet I knew he would live a long, prosperous life – if only to spite me.

Eventually a certain tension grew between us. I could not hide my frustration and dislike of her father. Lucy betrayed her frustrations and the strain in her letters (we are far too English and repressed to talk about things openly and passionately in person, thank God). She asked if I could somehow earn more money – perhaps by writing a novel. She also dared to communicate one of her father's opinions, that if I was serious about the relationship then I would somehow find more money or make sacrifices.

The wedding and cricket season were upon us - and I lacked dates in the diary for both. Until Raffles returned.

Chapter Three

My spirits soared - and not just because I saw a large, shining gin and tonic upon the table. From the measure and number of ice-cubes contained in the glass I knew that my friend had returned. I had popped into the Albany to collect Raffles' mail and check that all was well with his apartment – that the cleaner had been and the staff of the building had replenished the candle upon Raffles' desk.

"You're allowed to drink it old chap, rather than just stare at it," my long absent friend exclaimed as he came into the room. At first I merely stood there, my mouth agape. He had been gone so long I must have looked like I was seeing a ghost. Part of me wanted to chastise my friend like a mother would her unruly son for his sudden departure and intermittent contact, but I could not help break into a smile. I first shook his hand vigorously – but then I embraced him. Should I have been able to drink one or two large gin and tonics beforehand then tears may have even streamed down my cheeks.

Raffles lit a Sullivan and poured himself a whisky and soda-water. A sun-kissed complexion now accompanied the twinkle in his eye and he looked a picture of health and happiness, albeit I knew all too well how dramatically Raffles could retreat into the shadows and sink into a gloom. I shot out half a dozen questions about why he had left and what had he been up to these past four months, without pausing to give my friend time to answer. But he merely waved his hand dismissively – or he wished to wave away the growing cloud of cigarette smoke between us – and said that he would share his escapades on the continent another time. He was far more interested in how I was.

I recounted how my relationship with Lucy had continued to blossom over the previous few months, but I also unburdened myself in regards to her father's treatment of me and the dismal prospects of my ever being able to marry the woman I loved.

"I remember meeting Lucy's father in Truro. His company was as disagreeable as his claret. All he wanted to do was talk about money – and judged each man according to how much capital he had in the bank. I considered him to be morally bankrupt then. After his treatment of you Bunny, he's endeared himself to me even less. His second love, after lording his wealth over people, is cricket, if I remember rightly. You may well be able to gain some currency with him old chap through the game. He possesses his own team, of both gentlemen and players. He mentioned in passing once how he would be willing to pit his team against any I could assemble. Perhaps we should take him up on his offer," Raffles pronounced, with a sly grin on his face. Although such a grin usually bespoke of future peril, I had missed seeing it all the same.

"What are you intending to do?" I asked, partly worried and partly excited.

"My dear Bunny, I'm going to get you to the church on time."

Chapter Four

Raffles was a whirlwind of activity, for once, over the next week or so. He first contacted Prescott Rosebery to arrange a date and the ground rules for the match. We would play the game in a village just outside of Truro. Raffles suggested that the match should be followed by a dinner between the players. Raffles even offered to lay on a picnic for Rosebery's staff too, so they could enjoy the event. Perhaps fearing that Raffles would recruit the likes of Ranji and C. B. Fry to his team, Rosebery suggested that Raffles should only be able to pick players from the schools and colleges that he had attended - or rather that we had attended.

"Is he proposing that I play too, then?" I said, nervously gulping after I asked the question.

"Yes – and for once I'm in agreement with him. You will thank me too for having you play a part in his downfall."

"But you know how I'm more likely to catch a cold than the ball. I wouldn't want to let the team down."

"I have faith that you'll let neither the team nor yourself down, Bunny. You will, after all, be our Captain."

I gulped, again.

"You do know that Prescott will field a strong side? His team consists of gentlemen and players who have batted for the county – and even country in some instances."

"I have been in continual practise. I shall win at the odds," Raffles replied, quoting Hamlet and smiling. I thought him mad, believing that he could defeat Prescott's team with just a bunch of our old class mates – but only mad north north-west. Raffles was Raffles – and I sensed that he already had a semblance of a game plan.

Raffles made a few telephone calls and sent out numerous telegrams and letters to former school friends. Most were only too pleased to receive his invitation to play alongside one of the greatest spin bowlers of the age. We had eight confirmed players a few days before the date of the match. Raffles said that he was still waiting upon one "special" player. It had been agreed beforehand that any shortfall could be made up from locals from the village. I suspected that there were quite a few chaps in the area who would jump at the chance to help bring their landlord down a peg or two.

Chapter Five

Raffles and I travelled down to Truro a day before the match. Thankfully we had a compartment to ourselves and I used the opportunity to try and quiz my friend about his time on the continent. Typically however he gave little away – although he wasn't wholly unforthcoming.

"And what of the rumour I heard that when you were in Vienna you had an affair with a ballerina?"

"Ah, you heard about Francine then? She danced out of my life as freely as she danced into it... It's a singular yet also ultimately underwhelming experience to hear Russian nihilists and anarchists talk about engineering a better society. It will be a society that will prove fair for all, yet fairer still for them in particular. Despite their folly and conceit, the Communists seem even more fanciful – and crueller... It seems to be the fashion in Paris at present that women should wear dresses that they are half falling out of. Yet in many instances by revealing everything they reveal nothing...,"

I duly asked if Raffles pulled off any jobs whilst away, to help fund his grand tour.

"Yes. I had to eat after all, Bunny – and Russian caviar and

French foie gras can prove expensive."

I must confess that I felt a pang of disappointment at not being present during Raffles' foreign escapades. Part of me wanted to ask if he had recruited an accomplice to help him with his jobs and share his adventures – but I was fearful of receiving an unwelcome reply. I also went fishing again as to why my friend had left the country so suddenly, but he didn't bite.

"I was worried when you left so abruptly, A.J.; especially when soon after I heard the news that Jack Shanks had been spotted in Paris. Were you not worried too?"

"No. I was not worried about Shanks taking his revenge. A man on the run needs friends more the enemies," Raffles replied, furrowing his brow upon espying a spot of mud upon his recently polished shoes.

"Did your leaving have anything to do with Irene Adler?"

I still recalled their parting, all those months ago. Irene had mentioned how she had once met a woman from Raffles' past, a "lovely woman". I witnessed a brief but haunting expression upon my friend's face. Raffles was not quite himself during the journey home – and indeed for several days afterwards.

"No. Irene Adler would have been a reason to remain in London, rather than leave. Wouldn't you agree?" Raffles remarked, arching his eyebrow and smiling. "You can blame John Milton for my absence. I found myself reading Lycidas again – and agreeing with him. "To morrow to fresh fields, and pastures new." I apologise for the nature of my departing though, Bunny. But I knew you would have insisted on accompanying me. I did not wish to sully your fresh fields and pastures new in regards to your relationship with Lucy. Of course, as you know, it also amuses me to keep you in the dark as to my actions," he said, with a twinkle in his eye. As if applauding his humour the train whistle sounded a couple of times.

Chapter Six

Lucy met us at the station. The ruby red dusk glowed as brightly as my blushes as she embraced and kissed me in front of Raffles. Yet her kiss and perfume electrified. If I did now write a novel to try and make my fortune, it would be about her. I was unsure about how much Lucy could or would emancipate womankind as a suffragette – but I felt she had emancipated me, from loneliness and the cobwebs of my past.

Prescott Rosebery had arranged a dinner for Raffles that evening, inviting some of the gentlemen (as opposed to players) that we would be up against the following day. Guests included Foster Campion, "a decent enough fellow but a mere flat-track bully when it comes to batting," Raffles remarked to me in private. Charles Simperton, the son of our host's business partner, recently back from America. He batted for the county, as well as for Prescott's local team. Lucy confessed to me how her father had harboured hopes that she might get to know Simperton better over the summer. If I had any fears that this favourite could become a rival suitor Lucy quickly put my mind to rest. "Such is his regard for himself that he'd probably wish to walk

Charles Simperton down the aisle, if he had the choice... The only book he reads is Wisden – and he confines himself to the sentences containing the words "Charles" and "Simperton" in that." Despite his daughter's dislike of the peacock, Prescott still arranged things so he was seated next to Lucy at dinner, though thankfully Raffles was at that end of the table and was good company for her. Alas, I was seated with the boorish Jamie "Jock" Campbell – "Scotland's best all-rounder", a title he gave himself, which scarce admitted of the lack of competition there was for the honour. I also sat next to the highly-rated wicketkeeper Henry Childe, who could catch anything – aside from the drift of the conversation. He spent half the evening obsessively straightening his cutlery and the other half muddling up his words.

"I saw you bowl once at Lords Raffles. I hope that doesn't give me an unfair advantage when it comes to batting against you tomorrow," Prescott Rosebery announced whilst the port was being served. Our smug host needed every unfair advantage he could get against Raffles – but I kept the thought to myself. A member of staff once confided to me how the bowlers in his pay – or those who he was landlord to on opposing sides – went easy on the old man. The result however was that the corpulent Captain had an inflated opinion about his abilities as a batsman. I feared that if Prescott Rosebery inflated himself anymore he would burst, or float away like a balloon. But again I kept the thought to myself.

"An unfair advantage is the least I can give you, in gratitude for such a wonderful meal this evening Prescott," Raffles replied, unruffled by Rosebery's attempts to intimidate him.

"I noticed that some of your team played for Oxford and Cambridge in their youth. But do you think that will be enough?"

"I will just ask that they give a good account of themselves."

"Hmmph. You should know that I will ask of my team that they win. Perhaps that's the difference between men like you and men like me."

"Let's hope that's not the only difference between us, Prescott."

"Hmmph."

"I'd never discount any team from winning with Raffles playing in it," Foster Campion here remarked, looking to temper his Captain's over-confidence and any rise in animosity around the two men.

"You're being far too gentlemanly, Foster. You should compare the entire team sheets, rather than just focus upon one name."

"One can never be too gentlemanly. One can, however, be too much of the opposite," I here inserted, unable to keep my thoughts to myself any longer. Our host here threw me a look borne from ire, or indigestion, but I remained in my crease and looked the bowler back squarely in the eye. It was one thing to try and belittle me, but I would not countenance him disparaging my friend.

"Well said, Bunny. A gentleman also knows how to win and lose with grace," Raffles added.

"There is no such thing as losing with grace."

A charming, glowing, enigmatic smile here appeared on Raffles' face, as if he were sharing a joke with himself. It was almost as if he was about to break out into laughter. Lucy looked at me quizzically, as if I could explain, but I merely shrugged my shoulders and look bemused. Indeed the entire table looked somewhat bemused.

"Perhaps you're right Prescott, perhaps you're right," Raffles replied, still smiling, sphinx-like.

Chapter Seven

Shortly after we finished with the port Raffles excused himself, saying he was going to take some air. Not wishing to overhear Prescott Rosebery extol the virtues – and financial assets – of Charles Simperton to Lucy any longer I decided that I needed some air myself. I ventured to the back of the house. I was expecting to find Raffles on the back porch, leaning against one of the columns, smoking a Sullivan and gazing out up at the clear night sky. The columns were expensively formed from Bath stone, albeit Prescott had painted them white. Some say there is no accounting for a sense of taste – but in the case of our host it was more so that there was no sense of taste to account for.

I decided to fill Raffles' place and leant against one of the columns. I could still hear the yammering of my fellow guests in the background, with our host doing his best to talk over everyone, but thankfully a swirling breeze and the nocturnal birdsong began to drown out the noise coming from the house. The scent of freshly cut grass and flowers scented the air, although I also drew in my cigarette smoke with an equal ardour.

I finally espied Raffles from the glow of his cigarette lighter.

My heart stopped, as I fancied I saw a face from our past in the darkness lean into my friend. Yet as the face was the last one I would have expected to find at such close quarters to Raffles, in such a way, I dismissed my fancy as just that, a fancy. The man was dressed in workman's clothing - and a flat cap shaded most of his face - to give further credence that my imagination was just running away from me. I warrant that my nervous disposition – and my disposition to drink more claret than I should – also fuelled my paranoia. No sooner had Raffles lit the man's cigarette than he disappeared back into the night. As Raffles walked back to the house I innocently asked who he had been talking to?

"Just a farrier that works here - who for a shilling and a light gave me some inside knowledge on our opponents."

"Did he tell you anything useful?"

"A few things. He mentioned how our host is not the best player of spin, which makes me think how I may well be able to make him look like the worst player of spin come tomorrow."

"Do you really think that we have a chance tomorrow, A.J? They are a strong team."

"To quote Milton again – and our old friend Mary Flanagan – "What good is strength without double the wisdom?""

Chapter Eight

It was later that evening when I discovered just how much courage Raffles had in his conviction that we could win. He was alone with our host in the drawing room. I was coming back from the bathroom when I caught the following exchange.

"Shall we make the match a little more interesting tomorrow? Would you care to make a wager on the outcome? Shall we say twenty pounds?" Rosebery proposed.

"The sum is fine, but I'm not sure if a mere financial wager will make things sufficiently interesting."

"I'm open to offers. I've complete faith in my team."

"Would you wager giving your blessing for your daughter to marry Bunny, should he ask for her hand?"

Prescott, no doubt puffing on a cigar, here coughed and spluttered. I nearly did so too, standing unseen behind the door.

"Are you being serious?"

"I must confess I'm seldom known for my seriousness, but in this instance I am indeed in earnest. Were you not in earnest about having complete faith in your team? Would you like to reduce the financial wager too?"

"I've still got complete faith in my team! She would probably say no to him regardless. What sort of name is Bunny anyway?! He merely amuses my daughter, that's all. When the time comes she will be sensible enough to realise that he could never support her and keep her in the style she is accustomed to, or that a Charles Simperton could provide. But if I were to make this wager, what would you bet on your side? Make me sufficiently interested in the stakes and I'll consider giving my blessing, should my team somehow not win the day."

"Well I cannot offer my hand in marriage, but I can offer you my spinning fingers. I will put myself at your team's disposal for this summer's cricket season."

Rather than react with excitement at having one of the greatest spin bowlers of the age play for his team, Rosebery's immediate response was to exclaim,

"I would be able to put up the ticket prices for the matches I arrange and promote."

I was here tempted to walk into the room and to condemn the wager as being absurd, or unfair, but I have to confess that the prospect of victory – and winning the chance to propose to Lucy – kept me selfishly rooted to my spot outside of the door, as much as I was uncomfortable about my friend potentially compromising himself for me.

I understandably slept little that evening. Waking nightmares and dreams plagued me as much as those that came whilst asleep. My fate would be decided upon the outcome of a cricket match. Not even the Beefsteak or Brooks' betting books contained such a proposition, I'd wager. I had to laugh, because the alternative was to cry.

Chapter Nine

I squinted up at an unblemished blue sky the following morning. Rain would not be stopping play. I was unsure whether to be pleased about this or not. Transport had been arranged to take the guests from the house to the ground but Raffles suggested that we walk over to the village green. It was a pleasant day and Raffles was keen to discuss the forthcoming match – and give me some pointers in private.

"Just block anything heading for the stumps, but feel free to swing your arms at any ball wide of them. I'm going to put myself in a little way down the order, so as to be at the other end whilst you're batting, old chap. I will have the measure of the pitch and their bowling attack by then. Just play with your head and heart, Bunny. Your best will be more than enough. There's more riding on this match than you might know."

I briefly raised a corner of my mouth in a wry smile. Finally I knew something that A. J. Raffles didn't think that I knew – and I was keeping him in the dark.

"Have you heard from our final player to say that he will be turning up?" I asked, still in the dark about something however.

"He will not let us down, I'm sure of it," Raffles replied, with a hint of anxiety - for once - in his expression which suggested that he might.

"Were you at school with him, or university?"

"Neither, although I briefly attended the same school as him, before I met you old chap. He is more than a couple of years older than me. Indeed rather than a fellow pupil, he was more like a teacher to me," Raffles said, whilst beginning to toss up a ball and catch it whilst walking, to help loosen his spinning fingers. The ball span rapidly, mesmerizingly, in the air each time.

"How good a player is he?"

"Oh, have no worries on that front. He's champion Bunny, veritably champion."

As soon as we got to the village green, which was also home to their cricket pitch, I looked for Lucy. Her hair shone golden in the sun. She was playing with some of the children from the village. She caught my eye and waved, offering me a smile of encouragement too; innocent of just how much was weighing on my mind and the forthcoming result. The rest of my life would somehow be lived in the shadows, her shadow, should I be unable to marry her.

It was now fifteen minutes or so before play would commence. An unforgiving sun baked my already glazed features. Still we were a player down and I began to wonder if we should recruit a local to fill our ranks. I had won the toss and, on Raffles' instruction, elected to bat.

"Best of luck," I remarked to the opposing Captain.

"When you have the best players, you have no need of luck," Rosebery curtly replied, sneering.

I had to concede that, for the most part, the opposing team did look to have the best players. Professional, athletic looking (aside from their captain) and well kitted out. My teammates were either quenching their thirst, via some West Country cider as opposed to water, or catching up with Raffles as he held court and they re-lived their school days. I began to regret my decision to miss breakfast. Worry had annulled my appetite earlier in the morning. Yet now my stomach felt queer - and a certain light-headedness came over me. I felt that all was lost – and not just in terms of the match - before the first ball had even been bowled. I recalled the first time that I had been introduced to Lucy, but the image receded. Blackness smothered my thoughts.

I passed out.

Thankfully, Raffles had already called for the Doctor.

Chapter Ten

A strong but gentle hand held the back of my neck, whilst another held the tumbler to my lips and poured a mixture of champagne and soda-water into my mouth. Fortunately the champagne was from the bottles that Raffles had arranged, rather than the fizzy vinegar inside the cases Rosebery had brought. I recognised my saviour immediately. His beard, which was now more grey than black, was perhaps even more well-known than that of Santa Claus. His familiar red and yellow MCC cap fit snugly upon his head. He wore a kind expression, every inch the considerate Doctor – as opposed to the fierce look of concentration he wore when he was at the crease. Lucy's angelic face was next to his. She even looked beautiful when fretful, I thought to myself.

"Raffles' plan was to make our opponents pass out with shock upon seeing me walk out to bat, not my own team captain," W.G. Grace remarked, with a boyish glint in his eye.

I smiled in response and soon recovered my senses, as otherworldly as the appearance of the Champion seemed. A crescendo of whispers and gasps swirled around the village green like a spring breeze. It was now time for my opponents to look defeated, without even the first ball having been bowled. Prescott had tried to remonstrate with Raffles, arguing that he was bringing in a "ringer" – but Raffles explained how he had briefly attended the same school in Gloucestershire as Grace and Foster Campion backed him up.

"Now, obviously it's up to you, Captain, but should you wish I'd be more than happy to open the batting."

"Yes," I replied, still a little in shock.

Raffles was now in view, wryly smiling. When a stern-faced Rosebery walked by him I heard him remark,

"When you have the best player, who needs luck?"

Shortly afterwards the good people of Truro were treated to the sight of the great man (great in terms of bulk and fame) walking out to bat. People cheered and clapped as if the Old Man had already scored a double century. His ability and achievements with the bat were second to none, and few could match his bowling prowess and averages when he was in his prime too. Grace once scored over eight hundred runs over an eight day period. He topped the batting averages for three decades. Thousands would turn out to see him, emptying the offices surrounding Lords and the Oval. Fry possessed more power, Ranji more elegance – but both would concede they still lived in the shadow of the Champion. Ranji went so far as to once write that Grace was responsible for re-inventing the art of batting,

"He founded the modern theory of batting by making forward and back-play of equal importance, relying on neither one nor the other, but on both... I hold him to be, not only the finest player born or unborn, but the maker

of modern batting... he turned its narrow straight channels into one great winding river."

I also remember Ranji's comment over a lunch at the Savile Club when discussing Grace and his batting, that he "made utility the criterion of style."

Yet, as much as he was a titan in regards to cricket, Grace was all too human. He was not devoid of flaws. A competitive spirit sometimes tipped over into deploying gamesmanship. As much one could argue he was worth every penny from the extra gate receipts he brought in, fellow players were critical of the separate fees he negotiated for himself for matches. Yet, if a charge of being mercenary could be brought against him, it should also be noted that Grace was generous, both with his time and money. He was greatly supportive of playing in benefit matches to help out fellow cricketers coming to retirement. Grace also possessed an endearing sense of humour, which could be both dry and mischievous. After the game that day a spectator and local club player asked Grace how to play a particular delivery, to which he wryly replied,

"I should say you ought to put the bat against the ball."

Chapter Eleven

From the very first over Grace commenced to put bat to ball. Raffles briefed our other opening batsman, Edward Bryce, to give his partner the strike as much as possible. Understandably Grace no longer possessed the athleticism of his youth but he found an extra yard of pace whenever he had to run a single to regain the strike. The fiercest balls were swotted away with ease. The champion played all around the wicket and treated the crowd to an array of shots. He soon passed his fifty. The bowlers seemed to be conflicted between admiration and frustration. A few overs after the fifty was up, Prescott Rosebery displayed his frustration by berating one of his bowlers, Alec "Shiny" Diamond, for being particularly expensive (albeit he was bowling a good line and length). Bryce later reported Diamond's response to his captain,

"I puts 'em where I likes, and he puts 'em where *he* likes."

It was far from a chanceless innings, but Grace made a century. He duly received an ovation from the crowd. I can still picture his sweet and grateful expression; he grinned and waved his bat as if it were the first hundred he had ever made. Grace was finally caught from behind on 115. The opposition's high was short-lived as when Grace came off they saw Raffles walk out from the pavilion. As the batsmen crossed I caught the following exchange.

"You owe me a dinner for this A.J."

"For helping to give someone their just desserts, I'll throw in a pudding too."

Now of course Raffles was renowned for his bowling, but when he concentrated and a match was in the balance, he could also hold his own with the bat. It also helped that he often practised in the nets with Ranji and Fry and looked to emulate their technique, as well as listened to their advice. He gave himself a couple of overs to play himself in and assess the bowling, but then the scoreboard began to tick over. It was no accident that Raffles often directed the ball in Prescott Rosebery's direction to score runs. The opposing captain was far and away their weakest fielder. It got to the point where the bowlers began to mutter at his mis-fields. It was Alec "Shiny" Diamond's time to feel frustrated. Sometimes he glared at his Captain, his hands on his hips, when the ball rolled beneath his fingertips. At other times he turned his back upon Rosebery and shook his head in disappointment, or disgust. It also got to the point where pockets of laughter sprouted out from the crowd, amused by the effort (or lack of effort) at the corpulent cricketer to stop the ball. He was soon drenched in sweat and bent over, forever puffing out his cheeks and catching his breath. No matter where he was fielding, Raffles would invariably play the ball to him at least once during an over. It was not before long when I joined him out in the middle. I scored a valiant twelve runs, a fair few of them at the expense of the opposing Captain's fielding prowess I'm pleased to say.

Raffles scored a half century and we managed a daunting 220 by the close of our innings. As we came off I noticed a number of the fielding team look hopefully to the heavens, either for the Almighty to help them with their batting technique against the bowling of Grace and Raffles, or to pray for rain. Should the Almighty have been present upon the village green however that day, he was batting for Harry "Bunny" Manders' team.

Chapter Twelve

After the break Raffles and Grace opened the bowling and removed the opening batsmen with little difficulty. Even when the game had effectively slipped away from our opponents I still chased down every ball in the field as if my life depended on it, which from a certain point of few it did. When I dived to stop a shot and returned the ball quickly to cause a run out I heard Lucy call out over the applause,

"O Captain, my Captain!"

I turned to see her face aglow with both pride and humour. My face, however, reddened to a colour resembling the cricket ball I had just thrown.

When the opposing Captain came out to bat Raffles volunteered to bowl a spell again. Rosebery's oiled bat glinted in the sunshine and he had changed into a new set of gleaming whites. He made a show of windmilling his arms, marking his crease and playing a few practise strokes when he made it to the middle. Those air shots however were the closest that Prescott Rosebery came to scoring a run that day. From the look in his eye I could tell that Raffles was up for some sport. I dare say that he could have taken

Rosebery's wicket immediately, but yet he wished to humiliate the bully first. The first ball he missed completely, with Raffles giving it air and beating the batsman in the flight. The second had zip and turn and bounced up on a full length to painfully strike Prescott upon his kneecap. The batsman first howled in agony and then comically hopped around his crease. The crowd were laughing in amusement, rather than sighing in sympathy. The third ball of the over again bamboozled the batsman, and he nearly fell back upon his own wicket. The fourth ball was the cruellest of them all, turning and snarling up to strike the unfortunate batsman in the groin. The game was delayed by five minutes. Should Prescott Rosebery somehow cut his daughter out of his will, there would be no new offspring on the horizon now after Raffles' last delivery I fancied. The batsman was a beaten man when he returned to his crease – and it was perhaps to his relief, as much as his disappointment, when the bowler's fifth ball of the over turned back sharply and uprooted his off stump.

Prescott Rosebery pursed his lips, held his head up high and puffed out his chest (albeit his stomach still protruded out more) but he knew that his pride and stature had been uprooted, akin to his off stump. People clapped and applauded Raffles and his bowling (he would never have to buy a drink in the village again) – but equally they were cheering the humiliation of their landlord. I almost felt sorry for the man. Almost, but not quite.

The opposing team were eventually all bowled out for 107. Any disappointment that the gentlemen and players of their team might have experienced was hopefully tempered by the consolation that they were bested by a team containing both A.J. Raffles and W.G. Grace. It was a match that they could tell their grandchildren about – and still feel proud.

So it was with few heavy hearts – albeit there were more than a few rumbling stomachs – that the teams came off the field to head to the large marquee, where they would sit down to a hog roast dinner.

"O Captain, my Captain," Raffles remarked, grinning, as he tossed me the match ball.

"Do you not want to keep it, as a spoil of war?" I replied, after catching the ball (for one of the first times in my life).

"You keep it, Bunny. Besides, I'm looking to take more than just a match ball off our host this weekend," Raffles remarked, with a twinkle in his eye that I knew all too well.

Chapter Thirteen

I looked over to the area on the village green where Rosebery's staff were having their picnic. I realised that Raffles had invited them all so he could have the house to himself. I was reminded of the episode contained in *Raffles: Stumped* when Raffles asked me to invite Alexander Cardinal to the Albany, in order to vacate his house and rob him.

Now you may wonder why I didn't here confront my friend and try to dissuade him from going ahead and robbing the man who may well turn out to be my father-in-law. But such had been the ill treatment I'd received from Rosebery over the preceding months that I gave the robbery my blessing, to the point where I was keen to somehow join Raffles and help him on the job. Prescott had constantly suggested that I should be more enterprising and get a second job. It was a shame that he would never know how I was finally heeding his advice, I thought to myself.

The cider, wine and conversation flowed. The sun continued to shine and there was a lovely, convivial atmosphere, for the most part, as all guests and classes happily chewed the fat – and crackling – with each other. The scene reminded me of a comment by a history student who I had recently met at the Savile. I think his name was Trevelyan.

"If the French noblesse had been capable of playing cricket with their peasants, their chateaux would never have been burnt."

Towards the end of the dinner Raffles gave a brief but entertaining speech, thanking the players and organisers for such an enjoyable day. He was even fulsome in his praise for our host. I heard Prescott Rosebery insert the odd "hmmph" during the speech, the loudest of which came when Raffles exclaimed (to the particular amusement of those who were around the dinner table the previous evening),

"There is no such thing as losing with Grace."

After delivering his speech and then going out to keep the cider and good cheer topped up for the picnickers upon the green, I thought that Raffles might then slip away. Desiring to join him on his excursion, I duly approached him during a quiet moment.

"Are you going to be heading off soon, A.J?" I asked, my face lined with a knowing smile and raised eyebrow.

"No, why ever would I do such a thing, Bunny? I intend to carry my bat, so to speak, until the end of the evening. Are you planning to head off however?" Raffles replied, a wry and suggestive smile lining his features too (I here feared that his smile was more knowing than mine).

The light was now fading, but lamps were lit. Still believing however that Raffles was intending to steal himself away – to subsequently steal other things – I kept my eye on my sly friend throughout the rest of the night. As well as my eagle-eye, Raffles was often followed around the room by Margaret Rosebery, a young cousin of Lucy's, who Raffles had a dalliance with last year. She had not lost any of her ardour for A.J. in his absence it seemed. He, however, appeared indifferent towards her advances.

When Raffles unassumingly slipped outside of the tent again I was quick to follow him. Yet, just as I was preparing myself to run to Prescott's house to catch Raffles up, should it come to that, I found him standing before me, calmly smoking a cigarette and glancing up at a bejewelled night sky.

"Hello old chap, in need of a smoke?" he asked, fishing out his silver cigarette case.

"No, I'm fine." A pregnant pause ensued before I leaned in to Raffles and whispered,

"Tell me straight, what are your intentions this evening?"

"Do you mean towards Margaret Rosebery?"

"What? No, of course not. Why, has she — but no matter. I mean what are your intentions in regards to the valuables left unguarded back at Prescott Rosebery's house?"

"I neither intend to lay a hand upon Margaret Rosebery, nor her uncle's valuables this evening, I promise you Bunny," Raffles replied, smiling again as if he were amused by a private joke to which only he knew the punch-line.

Chapter Fourteen

Later that evening I watched as one of Rosebery's gardeners breathlessly rushed into the tent and whispered something into his master's ear. I could tell that it was something serious, as Prescott put down his knife and fork and stopped eating. The colour drained from his face, as if he had been bled dry. I next saw him mouth the word, partly in disbelief, "Robbed?"

I desperately here cast my eyes around the room to make sure that Raffles was still at his table. He was. He was capable of defying the laws of the land, but not those of physics. I was certain he had something to do with events however, despite his cast iron alibi. A comical scene followed where our host passed out, attempting to clutch the tablecloth as he fell. Unfortunately his skills as a magician were on par with his batting abilities and he dragged to the floor all manner of plates, cups and cutlery along with the tablecloth. I rushed to Lucy's side in order to comfort her, as opposed to her father. Few were in the mood to continue the evening's festivities after news filtered through about the robbery. Rosebery's staff were ordered back to the house. Raffles volunteered to remain and help look after things this end. As much as part of me wished to remain with my friend, to question him about events which had just unfolded, I duly accompanied Lucy back to the house. She was genuinely distraught, as much for her father as for herself - and my shirtfront was damp by the end of the night from her burying her tear-soaked face in my chest.

When we got back to the house the family and staff alike began to assess the extent of the robbery. The safe had been located and cracked into. Lucy's jewellery box had remained untouched, but all other valuables and expensive ornaments had been taken. As well as being a professional cracksman it seemed that the thief had a trained eye, too, in regards to knowing which pieces of art to take. The two paintings that were absent from the walls were the two most valuable.

The shock to Rosebery's system was palpable. Several brandies accompanied bouts of anger, despair, dejection and, finally, resignation that all was lost. The police were called in but they failed to inspire a bout of hope. I stayed up late with Lucy and consoled her (as she in turn tried to console her father).

Rosebery remained resigned to his misfortune the following morning, yet rather than dejected he seemed more philosophical about the theft. He confessed how he was grateful for his wife and daughter being absent from the house when the burglar had struck. He also remarked how well I had attended to his daughter during the crisis.

"Perhaps you are – and will be – good for her Manders, after all."

Perhaps he was not such an awful human being as he was an awful cricketer I thought to myself, after all.

Chapter Fifteen

Thankfully, again, Raffles and I had a compartment to ourselves during our journey back to London – and we were scarce outside of Truro station when I questioned him about the events of the previous evening.

"Although I promised that I would not lay a hand upon Rosebery's valuables, I did not nor could not promise that nobody else would," Raffles remarked, with a look of satisfaction on his face derived from either his plan working out or the taste of his Sullivan cigarette. Maybe it was due to both.

"But how did you do it? Who was your new partner in crime?"

Raffles did not need to answer. The face of the figure that A.J. had provided a light for in the grounds of Rosebery's garden sparked in my mind again. It was Shanks!

The train continued to sing along the tracks as Raffles explained how he had returned to the Albany from dinner one evening after Christmas to find Jack Shanks, the notorious criminal and escaped prisoner, working his way through a decanter of Napoleon Brandy. Shanks would forgive Raffles for the bump on the head (see *Raffles: A Perfect Wicket*) – and for his stomach having to suffer prison food – if he would help him get out of the country. Raffles duly furnished Shanks with both a plan and funds. Once the two men had made it across to France however Shanks proposed they embark upon a Grand Tour of Europe – involving grand acts of larceny. Raffles would be able to open certain social doors and provide intelligence upon targets, for Shanks to then walk through those open doors - and open safes. "Wishing to distract myself – and indeed pining for some fresh fields and pastures new – I took Shanks up on his offer. It was all good sport for a time – and I learned a thing or two from my new business partner."

"So what did you come back for?" I asked, not a little jealous of Shanks for sharing in Raffles' adventures, in place of myself.

"It was not a question of what – but who, Bunny. And that who was you! A month ago I wrote to Lucy to ask how my best friend was faring. You seemed a little gloomy in your own correspondence. She intimated that something was troubling you, though she knew not what. I was a little curious and disappointed as to why you had not proposed to her, too. I grew concerned that somehow you may miss your chance with Lucy. As I said before, I want to get you to the church on time – and in style. The take from this haul should provide you with the necessary extra income to win Rosebery's approval. His own money should be good enough for him, no? Shanks of course owned some reservations about returning to the land where he is a wanted man – but I called in a favour. So too he is a romantic at heart - I explained your situation – and he could not resist the sport.

He was disappointed when I said that it would be our last job together however, but I explained how I already had another accomplice that I worked with in England. I'm hoping that you'll still be up for the job old chap, even when married. Work will be far more hazardous – and dull – without you."

"You know that I would follow you to the gates of hell – and beyond - A.J."

"Truro is far enough Bunny, Truro is far enough."

Chapter Sixteen

Reader, I married her.

I proposed to Lucy shortly after our trip to Truro. If I do say so myself I thought the manner of my proposal rather romantic and memorable. I arranged for a journalist friend of mine, Thomas "Arrows" Fletcher, to organise a specially printed front page of *The Telegraph*. We were on Westminster Bridge. The pre-arranged newspaper seller approached us and I purchased the special edition, with my front page attached, for Lucy. The newspaper seller handed her the copy and I asked what was on the front page? It read,

"Breaking News. Westminster Bridge. Occasionally impoverished writer Harry "Bunny" Manders asks the ever wonderful Lucy Rosebery to marry him."

Her eyes were wide open with shock and delight.

"Lucy, would you do me the honour of becoming my wife? I want you in my life – for the rest of my life."

"Bunny, you're my best friend. I love you, more than I thought I would ever love anyone. The honour would be mine, to become your wife," she replied, tears moistening her eyes, as well as mine.

We kissed.

True to his word, in regards with his bet with Raffles, Prescott did not refuse permission for me to ask for his daughter's hand in marriage. To break his word wouldn't have been cricket. I like to think that I had won Rosebery over somewhat and earned his respect too, but I can't be sure.

"Whatever makes Lucy happy will make me happy, too," he remarked, with more affection in his voice than in his expression.

What certainly made Prescott happy was my offer to pay for the wedding. He insisted that, as father of the bride, he should pay for things however. A compromise was reached by which we would both pay for the wedding, though technically – given that my contribution came out of my share of the robbery - a tradition was upheld and the bride's father paid for everything. Raffles however paid for an engagement party, which was held in the courtyard just in front of the Albany. He smoothed things over with the tenants of the building and Clarence, the ever obliging doorman, helped organise the event.

We were married in mid-summer. Raffles, Fry, Ranji and Thomas "Arrows" Fletcher all attended. Along with a few other guests they provided a guard of honour as we left the chapel, lifting their cricket bats above our heads instead of swords. Fry entertained the children at the reception afterwards by borrowing a wedding guest's walking stick and giving batting lessons, with an apple serving as a ball. His wife soon put a stop to his antics however, scolding him like a child whilst doing so. We received telegrams from Lord Rosebery, W.G. Grace, Iris Adams and even

Mary Flanagan. Doctor Watson also sent a telegram on behalf of Sherlock Holmes, which we decided not to read out as rather than sending best wishes Holmes reminded me of my promise concerning his Professor Moriarty – that we should get in touch immediately if ever we heard any news pertaining to him.

Raffles, of course, served as my best man and his speech, of course, eclipsed the one given by the father of the bride. A couple of "hmmphs" could be heard emanating from Prescott during the speech, whilst the rest of the room was bursting into laughter. At the end of the evening I heartily thanked my friend and shook his hand. He here embraced me though (usually I was the one who embraced him) and remarked,

"You are the dearest of friends and the best of men, Bunny."

Tears moistened both of our eyes.

That evening I spared a thought for Raffles – and I must confess that I felt sorry for him. I wished upon him the happiness that Lucy had brought into my life. I still knew so little about the affairs of his heart.

But Raffles was Raffles – and he was far too special a character for me to feel sorry for him too much. I pictured him returning to the Albany and lighting another candle upon his desk, keeping a flame alive for something, or someone. He would then pour himself a whisky and soda-water and open up his cigarette case and a good book. Or more so I pictured him by the fire studying the coming fixtures for the cricket season - planning his next match and, hopefully, our next job.

End Note

I would like to thank Matthew Lynn, Emily Banyard and all the team at Endeavour Press.

Should you be interested in reading more about W.G. Grace I can recommend Robert Low's *W.G. Grace: An Intimate Biography* and Simon Rae's *W.G. Grace*.

I feel like I have been on a journey these past months, to get both Raffles to the crease and Bunny to the altar. As well as being in the company of Raffles and Bunny I have increasingly felt that I have been in the company of you, the reader, on this journey. Thank you all for your comments and suggestions, both those spoken and written (from those in the UK and those outside of it). Please do keep writing to me, about Raffles or the other books. Although he is almost the opposite of Raffles, I would be interested to know if you enjoy the company still of Pat Hobby. Similarly, do get in contact should you have read the full-length novels of *Augustus: Son of Rome* and *A Hero of Our Time*.

I can be reached via richard@endeavourpress.com

Richard Foreman

ENDEAVOUR INK

Endeavour Ink is an imprint of Endeavour Press.

If you enjoyed *Raffles: The Complete Innings* check out
Endeavour Press's eBooks here:
www.endeavourpress.com

For weekly updates on our free and discounted eBooks sign up
to our newsletter:
www.endeavourpress.com

Follow us on Twitter:
@EndeavourPress